READING
Between the Lines

Non-fiction
Texts to Inform, Explain and Persuade

Published by Letts Educational
The Chiswick Centre
414 Chiswick High Road
London W4 5TF
☎ 020 89963333
📠 020 89968390
✉ mail@lettsed.co.uk
🌐 www.letts-education.com

Letts Educational Limited is a division of
Granada Learning Limited, part of the Granada
Media Group.

British Library Cataloguing in Publication Data
A catalogue record for this book is available
from the British Library.

Editorial, design and production:
Topics – The Creative Partnership, Exeter

Printed and bound in the UK

READING
Between the Lines

Non-fiction
Texts to Inform, Explain and Persuade

Contents

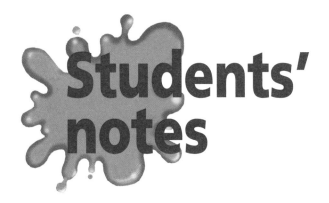

Students' notes

Welcome to a Key Stage 3 anthology of non-fiction texts. Yes, a whole book crammed full of factual writing. There are articles from newspapers and magazines, extracts from books and even a few contributions from the world of advertising. Some of the extracts may come from publications you know and others may be new to you.

To help you enjoy and investigate the texts further, there are some cunningly designed activities sprinkled liberally throughout the book. These will help you develop and practise those skills you have achieved with all the hard work you put into your Key Stage 2 Literacy hours. OK, there may have been a few bad days, a few moments of doubt, but they can't have been all bad because here you are in a Key Stage 3 English lesson about to enjoy reading and working on one of the texts. You may be doing this on your own or with a group, or maybe the whole class is trying to share a limited number of copies; whichever way you have been organised, there is so much in here that something is bound to catch your interest at some time.

In fact, you may want to revisit some of the texts as you progress through this key stage. Your experience of Key Stage 3 English will be part of your life throughout Years 7, 8 and 9, and you may find that you're using this anthology again in a different year because it has been written to include activities for all years at Key Stage 3. It is often interesting to discover how your reactions change as your literary horizons extend.

The activities in the **Read, Think and Write** and the **Read and Analyse** sections will help you understand the texts and develop your vocabulary, grammar and writing skills. The **Read, Discuss and Act** section will give you a chance to talk about and act out issues that arise from the text.

The contents of the anthology have been carefully chosen to provide a wide variety of informative texts, recounts, explanations and instructions. There are also examples of persuasive and discursive writing. By using examples of writers' work as models, the anthology may help you develop your own writing skills and your ability to express and communicate your own ideas.

I hope the book provides you with some moments you enjoy.

Teacher's notes

The aim of the anthology is to provide a wide variety of texts which could be used for individual study, group reading activities or whole class interaction. An anthology is by its very nature something to dip into, so it has been designed to offer a good measure of flexibility.

There is some differentiation in the way the book is organised to enable teachers to plan their work. Each of the six sections contains texts and activities suitable for Year 7 through to Year 9. The texts have been chosen to provide examples of non-fiction material which has links with different subjects across the curriculum. The work will help students develop and practise the skills of analysis they will have experienced with short sections of text in their Key Stage 2 Literacy work. It is also intended to lead them towards the demands of the texts they will work with at Key Stage 4. The focus or theme of each section is based on the learning objectives of the Key Stage 3 Literacy Framework.

- Information texts to display how information is organised and linked.

- Recounts to show the use of past tense, clear chronology and temporal connectives.

- Explanations to show the use of present tense and impersonal voice and logical and causal connections between points.

- Instructions to show sequence and the deployment of imperative verbs providing clear and concise guidance to the user.

- Persuasion – to display the methods of emphasis of key points and the articulation of strong logical links in argument.

- Discursive writing – to show the organisation of contrasting points and clarifying the viewpoint expressed.

The activities have been grouped into three sections and again, to facilitate planning, each section is focused on the learning objectives of the Key Stage 3 Literacy Framework. The **Read, Think and Write** section contains activities to support a student's grasp of meaning within a text and follows the objectives of the Text level Reading and Writing element of the Literacy Framework. The activities in the **Read and Analyse** section enable a student to practise and develop Word level and Sentence level work. The final section, **Read, Discuss and Act**, provides questions for discussion and drama activities which will ensure that students experience some of the Speaking and Listening objectives in the Framework.

As with all Key Stages, the spectrum of ability and interest at Key Stage 3 is wide, but the flexibility of this anthology in its choice of texts and the organisation of its activities will enable it to be fitted into a school's English curriculum to provide a stimulating and literacy-focused resource.

Note The extract from the Amnesty International book contains a photograph of a public execution that may be disturbing for some readers. Teachers are advised to look carefully at this before deciding whether to use the extract with their class.

CAMBRIDGE
THEATRE COMPANY

Bernard Shaw

Arms and the man

BP

Sponsored by British Petroleum

front

back

CAMBRIDGE ARTS THEATRE   15–25 JANUARY 1992
BOX OFFICE: (0223) 352000

Performance times:
Evenings 8pm, Saturday matinees 2.30pm

Ticket prices:
Monday–Thursday evenings £7.50, £8.50, £9.50
Friday and Saturday evenings £8.50, £9.50, £10.50
Saturday matinees £6.50, £7.50

Discounts:
Wednesday 15 January: Friends
Thursday 16, Friday 17 and Monday 20–Friday 24 January
and Saturday matinees: £6 savers in advance and £5 standby
1 hour before the performance for children under 16, UB40
holders, OAPs, students, registered disabled.

Party Discounts:
School parties of 10 or more: all tickets at standby rate and
1 seat in 10 is free. Adult parties of 10 or more: 10% discount
off all tickets.

Telephone Booking: (0223) 352000
Box Office open: 10am–8pm Monday–Saturday (until 6pm on
non-performance days).

Postal Booking:
Box Office, Cambridge Arts Theatre, 6 St Edward's Passage,
Cambridge CB2 3PL.

Accessibility: Cambridge Arts Theatre has an infra-
red system for people with impaired hearing and
limited access for wheelchair users. Please enquire in advance
at the Box Office.

Transport: Cambridge Arts Theatre is in the centre of
pedestrianised Cambridge – central parking is available but be
sure to allow plenty of time.

*Sign language interpreted performance on Saturday
25th January at 2.30pm*

Programme and background information, concept
and storyline available on audio cassette – telephone
(0223) 357134 for further details.

Cambridge Theatre Company Education provides workshops and written
background material to accompany each production. For more information,
contact Andy Holland on (0223) 357134

Cambridge Theatre Company is funded by Cambridge City Council and
Cambridgeshire County Council.

Designed by Ab creative, Cambridge

10

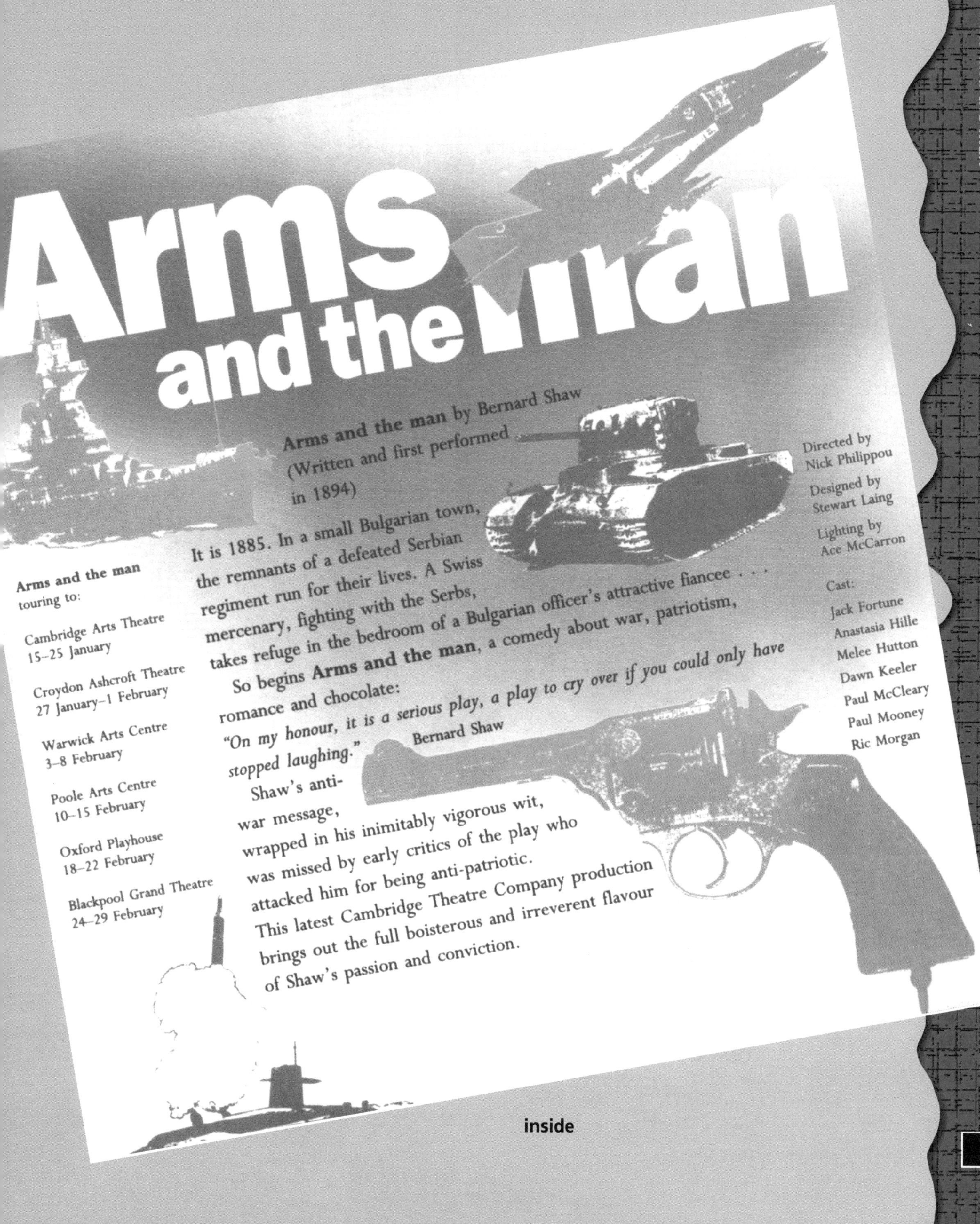

Arms and the man

Arms and the man by Bernard Shaw
(Written and first performed in 1894)

It is 1885. In a small Bulgarian town, the remnants of a defeated Serbian regiment run for their lives. A Swiss mercenary, fighting with the Serbs, takes refuge in the bedroom of a Bulgarian officer's attractive fiancee . . . .

So begins **Arms and the man**, a comedy about war, patriotism, romance and chocolate:

"*On my honour, it is a serious play, a play to cry over if you could only have stopped laughing.*"
Bernard Shaw

Shaw's anti-war message, wrapped in his inimitably vigorous wit, was missed by early critics of the play who attacked him for being anti-patriotic. This latest Cambridge Theatre Company production brings out the full boisterous and irreverent flavour of Shaw's passion and conviction.

Arms and the man
touring to:

Cambridge Arts Theatre
15–25 January

Croydon Ashcroft Theatre
27 January–1 February

Warwick Arts Centre
3–8 February

Poole Arts Centre
10–15 February

Oxford Playhouse
18–22 February

Blackpool Grand Theatre
24–29 February

Directed by
Nick Philippou

Designed by
Stewart Laing

Lighting by
Ace McCarron

Cast:

Jack Fortune
Anastasia Hille
Melee Hutton
Dawn Keeler
Paul McCleary
Paul Mooney
Ric Morgan

inside

front

CAMBRIDGE THEATRE COMPANY
PRESENTS

Abigail's PARTY

BY MIKE LEIGH

CAMBRIDGE
THEATRE
COMPANY

ARTS CENTRE
University of Warwick Coventry

University of Warwick, Coventry
28th January – 2nd February 1991
Box Office: (0203) 524524

Performance times
Monday – Friday 7.30pm
Saturday at 5pm and 8.15pm

Ticket prices
Monday – Thursday and Saturday matinee £7.50
(£5.95), £6.50 (£5.25)
Friday and Saturday evenings £8.50 (£6.50), £7.50
(£5.95)

Concessions
Children, Students, Senior Citizens, UB40 Holders,
Passport To Leisure Holders (Prices shown above in
brackets).

SIGN LANGUAGE INTERPRETED PERFORMANCE
AT 7.30 PM ON THURSDAY 31ST.

Designed by Ab creative, Cambridge

ARTS CENTRE
University of Warwick Coventry

University of Warwick, Coventry
28th January – 2nd February 1991
Box Office: (0203) 524524

Arts Council Funded

back

Abigail's
PARTY

Suburban London – Laurence and Beverly invite a few neighbours around for a sophisticated evening of drink and Donna Summer. But Ange, Tony and Sue get more than they bargained for when the lid is lifted off a bubbling cauldron of marital misery. Cigarettes, gin, olives, Dickens and death all play their part in this hilarious black comedy of a mismatched couple who love to hate each other.

Now recognised as a modern classic, *ABIGAIL'S PARTY* was first seen on stage and television in 1977 and fully established writer/director Mike Leigh's reputation as an outstanding talent. His later work includes *NUTS IN MAY* (for TV), the acclaimed *GREEK TRAGEDY* (which received its British premiere last year at the Edinburgh Festival and in London) and the award-winning feature film *HIGH HOPES*.

DIRECTED BY
Yvonne Brewster

DESIGNED BY
Martin Johns

LIGHTING BY
Simon Bayliss

CAST
Barbara Barnes
Doon Mackichan
Tony O'Callaghan
Mo Sesay
Anne White

Cambridge Theatre Company is funded by Cambridge City Council and Cambridgeshire County Council

...GAIL'S PARTY
...ing to:

...s Theatre,
...mbridge
...nd – 26th January

...rts Centre,
University of Warwick
28th January –
2nd February

Ashcroft Theatre,
Croydon
4th – 9th February

Opera House, Buxton
12th – 16th February

Towngate Theatre,
Poole Arts Centre
18th – 23rd February

Theatre Royal,
Winchester
25th February –
2nd March

Connaught Theatre,
Worthing
4th – 9th March

Theatre Royal,
Bury St Edmunds
11th – 16th March

Theatre Royal,
Glasgow
18th–23rd March

The Grand Theatre,
Wolverhampton
25th – 30th March

Grand Theatre,
Blackpool
1st – 6th April

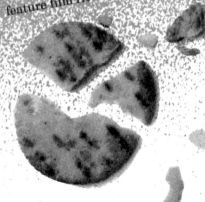

inside

Arms and the man leaflet
Abigail's Party leaflet

What do you need to know if you are planning a trip to the theatre? Having the correct information can be vital to making the evening's entertainment run smoothly. The two leaflets you have just looked at were produced to provide members of the public with information about the plays *Arms and the man* and *Abigail's Party*, as well as details of the performances at these particular theatres.

1. What part of the leaflet advertising *Arms and the man* gives the information you need for planning and organising a visit?

2. What information is given about tickets on the *Arms and the man* leaflet?

3. Why might it be best not to travel to this theatre by car?

4. Would people suffering from any particular disabilities be able to enjoy the evening at the theatre?

5. Look at the format and layout of the back of the leaflet for *Arms and the man*. How might this be improved? Would you:
   - edit the text?
   - alter the order in which information is presented?
   - change the headings?

   Explain the reasons for any changes you would make.

6. Write a summary in two paragraphs of the content and layout of the information which is shown in the inside section of the *Arms and the man* leaflet.

7. Look at the front of this leaflet. Make a list of the links between the front and the inside in terms of the information and the layout.

8. Write down your opinion of the use of illustration in both of these leaflets.

9. Who wrote *Arms and the man* and what is the play about?

10. Who wrote *Abigail's Party* and what is the play about?

1. Look at the synopsis of the play *Arms and the man* in the inside section of the leaflet. Use a dictionary and the textual context to help you write your own definition of the following words and phrases:
   (a) 'remnants of a defeated Serbian regiment'
   (b) 'a Swiss mercenary'
   (c) 'his inimitably vigorous wit'
   (d) 'boisterous and irreverent'
   (e) 'passion and conviction'
   (f) 'patriotism'

2. Design and write an information leaflet for either a play being put on at a theatre or a film being shown at a cinema.

1. With a partner or in a small group, compare and discuss the layout and content of the two leaflets. You could use the questions in 'Read, Think and Write' to help structure your discussion. Which design do you prefer and why? Do you think leaflets are an effective way of presenting information? If you were planning an evening out at the theatre, what other ways could you use to find out information?

2. The box office at a theatre or a cinema is the place where you can buy tickets or find out information about the current programme. In a small group, role-play a scene at a theatre or cinema box office. Use the setting to develop an assortment of characters that the person selling tickets and providing information might have to deal with.

Holiday hotel is shut in mass poison food fiasco

100 British tourists sue tour firms for thousands as sickness and diarrhoea ruin their vacations

BY DENNIS RICE

A HOTEL which appears in the brochures of some of Britain's biggest holiday firms has been shut following an outbreak of mass food poisoning.

The closure came after more than 180 British holidaymakers complained of sickness and diarrhoea after eating meals at the all-inclusive Barbados Beach Club.

One woman who returned to England has been diagnosed as suffering from salmonella.

Now up to 100 of those who had their holidays ruined are preparing to take up to six travel companies to court in a bid to win compensation. The action comes less than two years after 600 British holidaymakers fell ill from food poisoning at another all-inclusive hotel, Club Aguamar in Majorca.

The companies involved this time include Airtours, Thomas Cook, and the Upton Travel Group. Each stressed that they had stopped using the hotel the minute the problems came to light.

But Brenda Wall, of the consumer group Holiday Travelwatch, blamed the unusually high toll of sick holidaymakers on a lack of communication between the different firms.

She said: "Upton Travel had dozens of people keeling over there in February this year. Yet some companies were still sending people there in April until all their people started

VICTIMS: Jeannette and Dennis Worster fell ill after eating the all-day buffet at the Barbados Beach Club where birds swooped on food

falling ill as well." She also claimed that complaints from people who fell ill met with an unsympathetic response from both the various travel companies reps at the resort and the firms once holidaymakers returned home. "It would appear that legal redress through a group class action

for a personal injury claim is the only way forward," she said.

The International Travel Litigation Group, a Birmingham-based arm of solicitors Irwin Mitchell, has been instructed to pursue the group claim against the travel companies. Jeannette Worster and her

husband Dennis arrived at the resort earlier this year to celebrate their 20th wedding anniversary. They paid £2,030 to Upton Travel for a two-week holiday .

First Dennis, 67, succumbed to a violent bout of diarrhoea and vomiting which lasted 48 hours, then it was his wife's turn. Jeannette, 62, recalled: "I was in agony. I couldn't hold anything down. In the end I didn't eat anything for a week because I was afraid to."

Like other holidaymakers she blamed her illness on the main hotel's restaurant, where the all-day buffet has been identified as having been at the heart of the food poisoning outbreak. Staff were allegedly seen pouring water on ham to keep it warm and birds – notorious for carrying disease – were regularly seen swooping down on diners' plates.

Phodi Michael, a general manager with Upton Travel, which is based in Central London, said: "We ended our contract with the Barbados Beach Club the moment the problems began in February."

A spokesman for JMC Holidays said the company was currently settling compensation claims with seven customers.

TANNING: THE VITAL FACTORS

SUNCREAMS vary widely in price – from under £10 to well over £30 – and in the claims their producers make. But when it comes to effectiveness there is very little to choose between brands from high street chemists and more pricy makes like Piz, Buin and Nivea – apart from their aroma.

The effectiveness of the factor and its impact on the skin are almost exactly the same. But experts warn that many people do not understand sun factor ratings – wrongly thinking Factor 20 means they can stay in the sun 20 times longer – and many use far too little lotion.

Medical advice is that an average size man should use a third of a normal sized bottle per all-over application – or a bottle a day. The dangers are very real. In 1996, 40,000 people got skin cancer, twice the 1974 level and it kills around 2,000 people a year,

Holiday hotel is shut in mass poison food fiasco

100 British tourists sue tour firms for thousands as sickness and diarrhoea ruin their vacations

BY DENNIS RICE

A hotel which appears in the brochures of some of Britain's biggest holiday firms has been shut following an outbreak of mass food poisoning.

The closure came after more than 180 British holidaymakers complained of sickness and diarrhoea after meals at the all-inclusive Barbados Beach Club.

One woman who returned to England has been diagnosed as suffering from salmonella.

Now up to 100 of those who had their holidays ruined are preparing to take up to six travel companies to court in a bid to win compensation. The action comes less than two years after 600 British holidaymakers fell ill from food poisoning at another all-inclusive hotel, Club Aguamar in Majorca.

The companies involved this time include Airtours, Thomas Cook, and the Upton Travel Group. Each stressed that they had stopped using the hotel the minute the problems came to light.

But Brenda Wall, of the consumer group Holiday Travelwatch, blamed the unusually high toll of sick holidaymakers on a lack of communication between the different firms.

She said: "Upton Travel had dozens of people keeling over there in February this year. Yet some companies were still sending people there in April until all their people started falling ill as well." She also claimed that complaints from people who fell ill met with an unsympathetic response from both the various travel companies' reps at the resort and the firms once holidaymakers returned home. "It would appear that legal redress through a group class action for a personal injury claim is the only way forward," she said.

The International Travel Litigation Group, a Birmingham-based arm of solicitors Irwin Mitchell, has been instructed to pursue the group claim against the travel companies. Jeannette Worster and her husband Dennis arrived at the resort earlier this year to celebrate their 20th wedding anniversary. They paid £2,030 to Upton Travel for a two-week holiday.

First Dennis, 67, succumbed to a violent bout of diarrhoea and vomiting which lasted 48 hours, then it was his wife's turn. Jeannette, 62, recalled: "I was in agony. I couldn't hold anything down. In the end I didn't eat anything for a week because I was afraid to."

Like other holidaymakers she blamed her illness on the main hotel's restaurant, where the all-day buffet has been identified as having been at the heart of the food poisoning outbreak. Staff were allegedly seen pouring water on ham to keep it warm and birds – notorious for carrying disease – were regularly seen swooping down on diners' plates.

Phodi Michael, a general manager with Upton Travel, which is based in Central London, said: "We ended our contract with the Barbados Beach Club the moment the problems began in February."

A spokesman for JMC Holidays said the company was currently settling compensation claims with seven customers.

Foot-and-mouth

BY JOHN LICHFIELD
in La Baroche-Gondouin
STEPHEN CASTLE
in Brussels
AND MICHAEL MCCARTHY
in London

THE FIRST case of foot-and-mouth in France was confirmed yesterday, leading to an EU ban on French livestock exports and prompting America and Canada to block all European meat imports.

The growth of the foot-and-mouth outbreak into a worldwide crisis came as 22 new cases were confirmed in Britain – taking the total to 205 – and troops were put on standby to speed up the slaughter programme.

After the Continent's worst fears were realised when the virus was confirmed to have spread from Britain into a herd of 144 cattle at La Baroche-Gondouin in north-western France the European Union banned French livestock exports and the United States and

A French health service worker sprays hay with disinfectant on a road ne[ar]

INSIDE

Canada announced a block on all imports of live animals and meat products from the EU.

The EU said last night that about 90 countries have now imposed bans on EU livestock and meat products. The biggest importer, Russia, with about 40 per cent of the market, is still accepting products.

In addition, America, which represents about 10 per cent of the EU's market for animal products, will also confiscate all EU meat products imported in the past three weeks. Travellers to America will also be disinfected on arrival if they have come into contact with farms.

Countries across Europe were scrambling to put up barriers against livestock and food imports. As well as banning French livestock exports, the EU clamped down on the movement of farm produce within France itself.

The infected farm in France is next to another holding that had imported British sheep last month, before Britain's exports were banned. The entire herd had been slaughtered and would be incinerated, the French farm ministry said.

But to the horror of politicians and farmers alike, there were growing suspicions that the infection may already have spread.

The French Minister of Agriculture, Jean Glavany, warned that the disease may have been transmitted to other parts of the country in the last weeks of February.

France had imported about 20,000 sheep from Britain, at least half of which were now believed to have been carrying the virus, he said. "These sheep were dispatched to about 20 French *departements*, so they may possibly have transmitted the virus to others," Mr Glavany said.

A range of countries took unilateral action as soon as they received news of the French case, and before the EU's standing veterinary committee banned all French livestock exports.

Belgium, Ireland, Spain, Portugal and Poland announced bans on all hoofed animals from France. The Czech government banned hoofed animal imports from the whole of the EU, and the Dutch prohibited transport of cattle, pigs and goats in the Netherlands. The Italian government put foot-and-mouth controls on flights from French airports, and Germany told travellers not to bring back food from France.

Already batter[ed]
lapsing beef prices [by]
the BSE scare, farm[ers on]
the Continent were [facing]
the prospect of a s[econd eco]-
nomically devastati[ng]
Germany's de[p]

nic hits Europe

uin, north-west France, where foot-and-mouth has been detected *Reuters*

- ■ France confirms its first case of virus

- ■ EU bans all French livestock exports

- ■ British total reaches 205 after 22 new cases

- ■ US blocks all imports of EU meat products

- ■ Army on stand-by to speed up slaughter

inister, Alexander id: "Europe is now uly dramatic situa-1 Belgium's Farm aak Gabriels, said: tens us. We have to mmon reaction to-ffects everybody." ain, 22 new cases rmed, taking the UK 5 (including the sin-Northern Ireland). air held a series of vith ministers, farm d tourism chiefs at 0, which resulted in -up of a special task-be led by Michael an Environment examine the impact reak on the whole omy, and to "kick-

start" it once the crisis is over. Senior figures in the tourist in-dustry warned Mr Blair that rural areas reliant on earn-ings from visitors faced a dev-astating loss of revenue, and ministers agreed to recom-mend relaxing controls on foot-paths, open spaces and stately homes in areas judged free of the virus.

They are likely to include East Anglia, the Scottish High-lands and west Wales.

The Government said it would make a decision within 48 hours on the fate of up to half a million pregnant ewes and other livestock unable to get back to their home farms be-cause of the crisis: many may have to be slaughtered. The

Minister of Agriculture, Nick Brown, said he was considering bringing in the Army to help dispose of carcasses and to help slaughter livestock, al-though he rejected suggestions that snipers would be brought

in to cull wild animals. A second rendering plant is likely to open in the South-west.

Downing Street is playing down talk that the general elec-tion, expected on 3 May, might have to be postponed

Sunday Express article
Independent article

Newspapers are a source of information. They may be published in tabloid or broadsheet format and style. A tabloid newspaper is smaller and more compact in format than a broadsheet. Newspapers report facts about events in the world around us, but there may be comments and opinions about the facts within the reports. The first article you have just looked at is from the *Sunday Express*, a tabloid newspaper. The second article is from the front page of the *Independent*, a broadsheet.

Look at the *Sunday Express* article.

1. Who is the writer of the report?

2. What is the main idea in the headline and how and why is alliteration used?

3. What is the main idea in the first paragraph? What do you notice about the headline and the first paragraph?

4. What is the theme of the subheading and the second paragraph?

5. The article provides the supporting detail for three main ideas, which are in the headline and subheading. What are the three main ideas?

6. The writer uses a direct quote from Brenda Wall of the consumer group Holiday Travelwatch. What does she say?

7. Who else does the writer quote directly and what do they say?

Look at the *Independent* article.

8. Who is the writer of the report?

9. How many sub-headings does the article have?

10. Which of the main ideas in the headline and subheadings are repeated in the first two paragraphs?

11. Where in the article is the fifth sub-heading repeated?

12. Who is quoted directly in the article?

13. How many sentences are there in each of the first six paragraphs? Give examples of how punctuation is used within the sentences.

14. Use your own words to summarise each article in a paragraph of two or three sentences.

Read and Analyse

1. Use a matrix to investigate and compare the format and layout of the two reports. You could use the following headings:
   - Name and type of newspaper (e.g. tabloid/broadsheet)
   - Headline and subheading (e.g. number of subheadings, use of underlining)
   - Bullet points and lists (e.g. position in article)
   - Columns (e.g. number, length, variation in length)
   - Illustrations (e.g. number, size, position)
   - Paragraphs (e.g. number)
   - Text style (e.g. changes in type style and size)

2. Develop the matrix to investigate and compare other reports in a tabloid newspaper and a broadsheet newspaper. For example, you could look at the articles on the front page of each paper.

3. Using a newspaper style, write a report on one of the following items:
   - The opening of a new theme park
   - The result of a local council election
   - An accident in which a child falls from a bridge but is saved by a passing bungy jumper
   - A famous footballer admitting to a chocolate addiction

   Give the piece of writing a headline and a subheading but concentrate on content and style rather than layout.

Hint
Feature the main idea in the headline and repeat it in the text. Use short paragraphs. Give direct quotes from people involved.

Read, Discuss and Act

1. What types of information can you get from newspapers? Using a selection of newspapers, work in small groups to discuss how you might categorise the information.

2. In groups consider the following questions. Is a newspaper delivered or regularly brought in to your home? Do you read a newspaper regularly? Do you just read certain sections of a newspaper? Where else can people obtain the sort of information that is found in newspapers? Do you think we will need newspapers in the future? What effect do you think the internet will have on newspapers? Why do you think that newspapers are still read despite regular news reporting on television and radio?

3. Prepare and hold a debate on the subject: Newspapers v. the internet.

   One group should present the arguments in favour of newspapers, pointing out the positive advantages of printed material and the possible disadvantages of computer technology.

   Another group should present the arguments against newspapers, pointing out the advantages of computer technology.

Chapter 2
THE GREAT DETECTIVE

Sherlock Holmes may be world-famous but his career began modestly with *A Study in Scarlet*, first published in *Beeton's Christmas Annual* for 1887, and *The Sign of Four* (1890). His reputation was made by the short stories which appeared in *The Strand Magazine* from July 1891 onwards.

THE DEBT TO DUPIN

'You have been in Afghanistan, I perceive,' Sherlock Holmes remarks on first meeting Dr Watson at the beginning of *A Study in Scarlet*. Throwing out arresting little deductions about people on the basis of a casual encounter will turn out to be part of his stock-in-trade, as well as a natural consequence of his restless curiosity. It establishes his authority with clients – and readers too, of course – even before the case gets underway. But in *A Study in Scarlet* readers have to wait a chapter and a half, which Watson spends puzzling over the mysterious habits of his new flatmate and wondering what his profession might be, before Holmes reveals how he made the deduction about Afghanistan. Watson, he explains, has the look of both a medical and a military man, so he was no doubt an army doctor. He is suntanned, and he bears the mark of a recent injury. Where else could an army doctor then have seen active service in a hot climate but in Afghanistan?

The logic is compelling, or at least compelling enough to pass muster in a novel. But that is not quite how Watson chooses to put it:

'It is simple enough as you explain it,' I said smiling. 'You remind me of Edgar Allan Poe's Dupin. I had no idea that such individuals did exist outside of stories.'

Sherlock Holmes rose and lit his pipe. 'No doubt you think that you are complimenting me in comparing me to Dupin,' he observed. 'Now, in my opinion, Dupin was a very inferior fellow.'

This is in fact Conan Doyle's oblique way of paying tribute to Dupin's creator. Dupin disparaged his most famous predecessor, Vidocq, in a similar manner. For good measure Conan Doyle has Holmes continue with a few words dismissing Gaboriau's Lecoq as well: apart from his energy, the French policeman was, it seems, 'a miserable bungler' whose slow-wittedness could spin a case out to unnecessary length. That is more than a little unfair, particularly since *A Study in Scarlet* itself – like all the Sherlock Holmes novels except *The Hound of the Baskervilles* – unwisely follows Gaboriau in adopting a broken-backed structure which divides the narrative into two halves: the detective investigates and solves the case in the first, while the second gives a lengthy flashback of the past events which led to the crime.

Holmes is always at his best in the short stories. There, no reader could fail to be struck by how much Conan Doyle has borrowed from Poe and how happily he has enriched it. The debt begins with the central premise: a brilliant but eccentric detective who practises his own distinctive methods and an admiring friend who tells the story of their adventures together. Yet one only has to look at how Conan Doyle has transformed the character of the friend to appreciate the enrichment. Dupin's friend and chronicler does not even have a name: he is just a pallid version of Dupin himself, like Dupin in his nocturnal habits and his bookish tastes but without a genius for detection. After a

Examining the body of the victim in *A Study in Scarlet*: a bowler-hatted Holmes (above), portrayed by George Hutchinson, and a top-hatted Holmes, by James Greig.

shaky-sounding start under the dandified name of 'Ormond Sacker' in Conan Doyle's notes for *A Study in Scarlet*, Watson quickly becomes distinctive in his own right, as Holmes' temperamental opposite: solid in his conventionality, his predictability and his loyalty, his average intelligence untouched by imagination or genius. It is as impossible to imagine Sherlock Holmes without Dr Watson as to imagine Cervantes' Don Quixote without Sancho Panza or Dickens' Mr Pickwick without Sam Weller.

The possibilities latent in this marriage, or mismarriage, of opposites sustained Conan Doyle in giving his creations a far longer career than Poe ever gave his. Poe published three stories in four years. Conan Doyle published four novels and fifty-six short stories over some forty years. And he announced his transformation of the bloodless and theoretical world of the Dupin stories even as he deliberately invoked the memory of them in that early exchange about Afghanistan. Holmes' description of Dupin as 'inferior' – others might have called him insufferable – signals the arrival of not just another genius on the scene but another arrogant genius. His arrogance, however, makes him potentially comic in a way that was inconceivable of Dupin. All Poe's jokes

(never very funny and sometimes gratingly unfunny) are at the expense of Dupin's detractors, but Holmes himself has just been made the butt of a joke that will run and run throughout his adventures. When he explains how he has reached one of his startling deductions, he is always liable to receive not the admiration which greets Dupin but the reaction conjurers get when they explain how they pulled the rabbit out of the hat: it's easy when you know how it's done.

From the start, then, Conan Doyle located Holmes in a human and social comedy which has room for sly little jokes. He soon realized that the essence of such jokes does not stale with repetition, and he added various familiar routines to his stock: the moments when Holmes' vanity is wounded by compliments to his greatness failing to materialize, for example, or when Watson's hope that he

Holmes and Watson on their way to Dartmoor to investigate the disappearance of the racehorse Silver Blaze. Illustration by Sidney Paget for *The Strand Magazine*.

has learned to imitate Holmes' methods is dashed yet again. As time went by, Conan Doyle found room for affection, too. The early Holmes can be savage in his contempt for Watson's ineptness at detection, but the late Holmes comes close to tears when his friend is wounded. Affection had no more place than good jokes in the coldly intense atmosphere of Poe's art, but jokes and affection are as much a part of the fabric of the Holmes

stories as mysteries and their solution. Quite as much as the plots, these are what have made the stories endure.

ART AND REASON

The forty years Conan Doyle spent writing the Sherlock Holmes stories brought about more changes than a growth in affection between, and sometimes towards, his characters.

This was inevitable, if only because when he first conceived Holmes and Watson he had no means of knowing their adventures would grow to such proportions. When he wrote *A Study in Scarlet* he was still a young man, struggling in both his chosen professions as author and doctor. The novel attracted little notice, either on its appearance in *Beeton's Christmas Annual* in 1887 or on its reappearance in book form the following year, and Conan Doyle had every reason to suppose he was finished with Holmes. It was only the accident of a contract from the American publisher Lippincott which revived the detective for a second novel, *The Sign of Four* (1890).

Success came with the first series of short stories for *The Strand Magazine*, collected as *The Adventures of Sherlock Holmes* (1892). But by the time of the second series, collected as *The Memoirs of Sherlock Holmes* (1894), he had resolved to get rid of Holmes and invented Professor Moriarty for the purpose in 'The Final Problem'. Popular outcry, coupled with lavish financial offers from publishers, made him first produce *The Hound of the Baskervilles* (1901–02), an adventure set retrospectively before Moriarty's arrival on the scene, and then bring Holmes back from his watery grave at the Reichenbach Falls in 'The Adventure of the Empty House', the first of the stories collected in *The Return of Sherlock Holmes* (1905). Thereafter Conan Doyle turned intermittently and with professed reluctance to Holmes, like a man at once adding afterthoughts to a national monument and making deposits in his pension fund. The results were a novel, *The Valley of Fear* (1914–15), and two more collections of the stories which *The Strand Magazine* continued to publish, *His Last Bow* (1917) and *The Case Book of Sherlock Holmes* (1927).

Holmes awaits the final confrontation with Professor Moriarty at the Reichenbach Falls. 'It was the last that I was ever destined to see of him in this world,' wrote Watson, not foreseeing that Holmes would come back to life for further adventures. Illustration by Sidney Paget to 'The Final Problem'.

There is a scholarly treatise yet to be written on the relationship which can develop between a writer and a character invented for a specific occasion but retained as a series character and grown into a near-lifelong companion. The history of detective fiction is particularly rich in examples: the names of Maigret and Lord Peter Wimsey immediately add themselves to the list which begins with Holmes. Weariness and impatience prevented Conan Doyle from simply growing old gracefully with his creation, as Simenon did, or trying to turn two flimsy dimensions into three solid ones, as Dorothy L. Sayers did. But he could not resist the obvious temptation (countless later writers have surrendered to it as well) of making his character more and more resemble himself. Inevitably, that meant making Sherlock Holmes nicer.

Despite the genial comedy which crept in from the start of *A Study in Scarlet*, Conan Doyle originally conceived his detective as a cold fish, in much the same way and for much the same reason that Dupin is a cold fish. When he does eventually get round to telling Watson he is 'a consulting detective', Holmes presents himself above all as the exponent of a theory and the practitioner of a method of detection. These do not require the sort of elaborate introductory essay Poe offered at the beginning of 'The Murders in the Rue Morgue' because they were less original to Conan Doyle and more familiar to his readers. The theory is essentially the theory of scientific rationalism, the method that of diagnostic medicine. Conan Doyle himself had learned both in his time at the University of Edinburgh, where he had been particularly impressed by Dr Joseph Bell, whom he no doubt had in mind as a rough model for Holmes when he sat down to write *A Study in Scarlet*.

A Hard-Boiled Dictionary

The slang in use among criminals is for the most part a conscious, artificial growth, designed more to confuse outsiders than for any other purpose, but sometimes it is singularly expressive...

Dashiell Hammett 'From the Memoirs of a Private Detective' (1923)

I'm an intellectual snob who happens to have a fondness for the American vernacular, largely because I grew up on Latin and Greek. I had to learn American just like a foreign language. To learn it I had to study and analyse it. As a result, when I use slang, solecisms, colloquialisms, snide talk or any kind of off-beat language, I do it deliberately. The literary use of slang is a study in itself. I've found that there are only two kinds that are any good: slang that has established itself in the language and slang that you make up yourself. Everything else is apt to be passé before it gets into print.

Raymond Chandler letter of 18 March 1949

BADGER GAME - blackmail practised on a man who is lured by a woman into a compromising situation and then threatened by her male accomplice

BANG-TAIL, PONY - racehorse

BEAN-SHOOTER, CANNON, GAT, HEAT, HEATER, ROD, RODNEY, ROSCOE - gun (usually pistol or revolver)

BEEF - to grumble

BERRIES - dollars

BIG HOUSE, CABOOSE, CAN, COOLER, HOOSEGOW, PEN, STIR - jail (see also BOOBY HATCH)

BIG ONE, CHICAGO OVERCOAT - death (THE BIG SLEEP was Chandler's own coinage, which he lived to see used by Eugene O'Neill in THE ICEMAN COMETH in the belief it was genuine gangster slang)

BIRD - guy (also YEGG)

BLIP OFF, BLOW DOWN, BOP, BUMP, BUMP OFF, CROAK, KNOCK OFF, POOP, POP, RUB OUT - to kill (BOP also = to punch or hit)

BOOB - fool (also MUG, RUBE, SAP)

BOOBY HATCH - psychiatric hospital or jail

BOOZE HOUND, JUICER, LUSH, SOUSE - alcoholic

BOP, SOCK - to punch or hit

BRACE - to grab

BRACELETS, CUFFS, NIPPERS - handcuffs

Cont...

RAYMOND CHANDLER: A QUALITY OF REDEMPTION

Chandler consolidated what was immediately usable in Hammett's achievement in the sequence of seven novels about Philip Marlowe that he began, some five years after Hammett had stopped writing, with *The Big Sleep* (1939) and finished, though less with a bang than a whimper, with *Playback* (1958). In particular, he took the Continental Op stories and *The Maltese Falcon* as his points of departure, elaborating the private eye Hammett had sketched with such neutral dispassion into an icon, easy to recognize and easy to admire. The bored afternoons in his dusty office when Marlowe opens the bottle in his desk drawer, the evenings he spends playing chess with himself in his apartment, the late-night phone calls that take him out on the latest stage in a case: Chandler makes these familiar routines. The city where Marlowe works becomes equally familiar, with its geography of contrasts between the smart apartments of the rich and the cheap hotels or rooming-houses of the failed. That geography, too, has its roots in the world Hammett evoked, though Chandler sharpens the contrast by adding more corrupt glitter and more pathetic seediness.

Everything, indeed, seems to have been sharpened in Chandler's world. It appears more vivid than Hammett's and promises, even on its introduction, to prove more memorable. Where Hammett's prose was bare and laconic, Chandler's is deliberately heightened. 'He had style, but his audience didn't know it,' Chandler said of his predecessor, knowing full well that nobody could fail to notice he had style. It was the dullness he most objected to in Golden Age fiction, the dullness of writers who loved

reader, Chandler presents pathos or corruption with those labels already attached. His vision is avowedly moral from the start of the narrative; solving the mystery and resolving the plot at the end will merely affirm the specifics, the technicalities of guilt or innocence. And since Marlowe is both narrator and detective, he occupies a special position as an authority not just on mysteries but on the society in which the mysteries happen.

In practice, this means that he has a code for living honourably as well as for doing a reasonably honest job as a private detective on a case. And it means that the code is a basic premise on which the novels depend, not (as in Hammett) something to be discovered in the course of the narrative and still open to challenge once discovered. Chandler states this as plainly as the language of hard-boiled fiction allows on the first page of *The Big Sleep*. Marlowe arrives at the Sternwood mansion for the interview with General Sternwood which begins the case. Left by the butler to wait in the empty hall, he notices a stained-glass panel showing an Arthurian knight who has presumably just killed the dragon and is freeing the maiden from the ropes tying her to a tree:

I stood there and thought that if I lived in the house, I would sooner or later have to climb up there and help him. He didn't seem to be really trying.

At first reading his remark sounds faintly like a leering joke about the pleasures of grappling with captive maidens – and certainly, leering jokes do play their part in the queazy sexuality which the novels go on to discover in Marlowe. But the remark is not just a joke. The plot about to unfold will involve dragons and maidens, and Marlowe's role will be that of Arthurian

thinking up plots but did not actually like writing. He applied himself conscientiously but without enthusiasm to the business of plotting and kept his real energy for the local intensity of the narrative: turning a passing character into an immaculately observed thumbnail sketch, a scene briefly glimpsed into a sharp vignette.

Yet the heightened effect of Chandler's work comes from something more than the sheer energy and care he put into his writing. Its vividness is not just that of things and people seen, but of things and people confidently assigned their place in a moral scheme. Where Hammett had been content to leave judgement to the

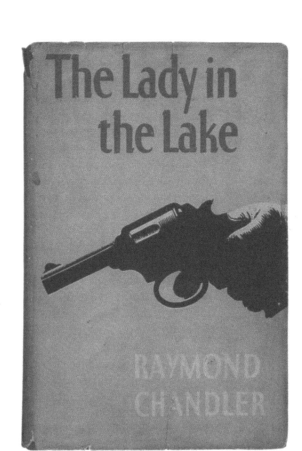

knight. Chandler had, after all, originally thought of naming him Malory. Making detection into a form of knight errantry, chivalry in action, was by no means a new idea when he wrote *The Big Sleep*: several Victorians had done it and so, more memorably, had Conan Doyle. What is remarkable about Chandler is the way he makes the idea look fresh and appropriate in its urban Californian setting.

Finding dragons and captive maidens in California proves no problem, though often Chandler's maidens turn out to be more dangerous than the dragons. His task is further eased by the way the 'open' form of hard-boiled narrative already resembles the quest: a journey and a series of encounters on the way to an ultimate goal. In Arthurian romance these encounters serve a double purpose, giving

the knight an additional pointer to his route and testing his virtue, his fitness for the journey. The confrontations which make up the plot of Chandler's novels serve exactly the same double purpose. Chandler ritualizes the process, as he does the routines which make up Marlowe's daily life, and emphasizes what is unpromisingly shabby about his hero. Sam Spade at least had a partner and a loyal secretary, but Marlowe, merely because he is a private detective, is small-time and apparently almost friendless.

It was Chandler more than any other writer who established the convention that private detectives in fiction should be marginal, if not despised figures. Their bank accounts are low and their cars unreliable. Their clients lie to them and try to manipulate them. The rich people they deal with regard them with open contempt; even the poor react with sullen indifference. The police are often hostile, sometimes eager to pull their licence to operate and sometimes just brutal. Everywhere they go, private detectives are treated as people to be bought, to be used, to be leaned on. Marlowe endures these ordeals, living in a world where the common slang terms for people of his profession – 'shamus', 'peeper' and the rest – almost all carry a sneer. 'So you're a private detective,' Vivian Regan greets him in *The Big Sleep*, 'I didn't know they really existed, except in books. Or else they were greasy little men snooping around hotels.' 'A private detective,' ponders a visitor to his office in *The High Window*. 'I never met one. A shifty business, one gathers. Keyhole peeping, raking up scandal, that sort of thing.'

Marlowe triumphs not just eventually in solving the case but stage by stage, like the knight on his journey. In a society where money and power are almost always in the hands of the morally suspect, the shabby job, like the shabby office, becomes an emblem of the essential purity underlying his toughness. And, of course, he carries his toughness not in his fists but in his language. Interviews, which in the hands of other writers might be (and frequently are) just routine exercises in getting the details of the case across to the reader, come alive with wisecracks. His client in *The High Window* tells him: 'I don't think I'd care to employ a detective that uses liquor in any form. I don't even approve of tobacco in any form.' He replies: 'Would it be all right if I peeled an orange?' A client complains about his manners: 'I don't mind if you don't like my manners. They're pretty bad. I grieve over them during the long winter evenings.' The gangster Eddie Mars resents being questioned in *The Big Sleep*:

'Is that any of your business, soldier?'

'I could make it my business.'

He smiled tightly and pushed his hat back on his grey hair. 'And I could make your business my business.'

'You wouldn't like it. The pay's too small.'

Chandler is always the most quotable of writers. But he also knew – unlike many of his imitators – that a hero and a novel cannot be built from wisecracks that sound amusing in isolation. They soon tire the reader or, worse, make the reader think the hero a smartass. Chandler's wisecracks work in context as well as out of it, showing how an apparently small man, without power or prestige, asserts his integrity and his code. Sometimes they help win Marlowe the respect or even friendship of those he talks back to, though on this point Chandler is uncertain and apparently indifferent. What matters is that Marlowe should keep the reader's respect and that, alone and powerless, he should begin his ordeal and triumph afresh in the next novel.

Marlowe reflects: a glimpse of Robert Montgomery as Chandler's private eye in the film *Lady in the Lake*.

The Crime and Mystery Book

by Ian Ousby

It is sometimes helpful to understand fiction texts by researching information about the writers. The extracts on the previous pages are taken from a book which looks at the development of the crime and mystery genre. Arthur Conan Doyle and Raymond Chandler were two famous crime writers. Conan Doyle created the character of Sherlock Holmes in 1887 and Chandler created the detective Philip Marlowe in1939. The extracts show how both writers developed their ideas and were influenced by the style and characters created by two other writers, Edgar Allan Poe and Dashiell Hammett.

1. What 'premise' did Conan Doyle borrow from Poe's writing?

2. How is Watson the 'temperamental opposite' of Holmes?

3. How does Conan Doyle develop the relationship between Watson and Holmes?

4. Who did Conan Doyle invent to get rid of Sherlock Holmes?

5. Why did Conan Doyle have to write 'The Adventure of the Empty House'?

6. Who did Conan Doyle use as a 'rough model' for the character of Sherlock Holmes?

7. What familiar routines does Raymond Chandler give his detective character Philip Marlowe in the novels he wrote?

8. Use quotes from the text to show the difference in style between the writing of Raymond Chandler and that of Dashiell Hammett.

9. How does Chandler establish the convention that private detectives in fiction should be 'despised characters'?

10. Use quotes from the text to help explain how Marlowe 'carries his toughness not in his fists, but in his language'.

11. The writers of 'hard-boiled' detective novels often used a style of slang. What is Raymond Chandler's opinion of slang and how did he contribute to its use?

12. Which character – Sherlock Holmes or Philip Marlowe – do you think sounds the most interesting in the way the writer has developed him? Use information from the texts to help explain your choice.

1. Use your own words to replace the underlined words in these sentences:

(a) 'Yet one only has to look at how Conan Doyle has <u>transformed</u> the character of the friend to <u>appreciate</u> the <u>enrichment</u>.'

(b) 'His <u>arrogance</u>, however, makes him <u>potentially</u> comic in a way that was <u>inconceivable</u> of Dupin.'

(c) 'Its <u>vividness</u> is not just that of things and people seen, but of things and people <u>confidently assigned</u> their place in a <u>moral scheme</u>.'

Hint
Read the sentences in context and use a dictionary and a thesaurus.

(d) 'It was Chandler more than any other writer who <u>established</u> the <u>convention</u> that private detectives in fiction should be <u>marginal</u>, if not <u>despised</u> figures.'

2. Find the meaning of these words from the texts and put them into sentences of your own:

evoked	manipulate
laconic	intermittently
premise	exponent
vignette	repetition
confrontation	deductions

1. Reference books and textbooks are used in schools as methods of providing information on different subjects. Are they generally successful in their aim? Do some subjects have better textbooks and reference books? Is this because of the type of subject or because of the way in which the information is presented?

2. Writers and designers often have to 'sell' their ideas to publishers or companies who will fund them, by giving a presentation. In a small group, prepare a 'package of ideas' for a book or series of books which provide the reader with information. Give a presentation talk in order to convince the publisher or company that your books are worth publishing or promoting. Remember that you need to refer to both the content and the design, so you may need to use some visual aids for your talk.

I woke up when the bomb came through the roof. It came through at an angle, overflew my bed by inches, bounced up over my mother's bed, hit the mirror, dropped into the grate and exploded up the chimney. It was an incendiary. A fire-bomb.

7

My brother Ivan appeared in pyjamas and his Home Guard tin hat. Being in the Home Guard, he had ensured that all the rooms in our house were stuffed with sandbags. Ivan threw sand over the bomb but the dry sand kept sliding off. He threw the hearthrug over the bomb and jumped up and down on it, until brother Pud arrived with a bucket of wet sand from the yard. This did the trick.

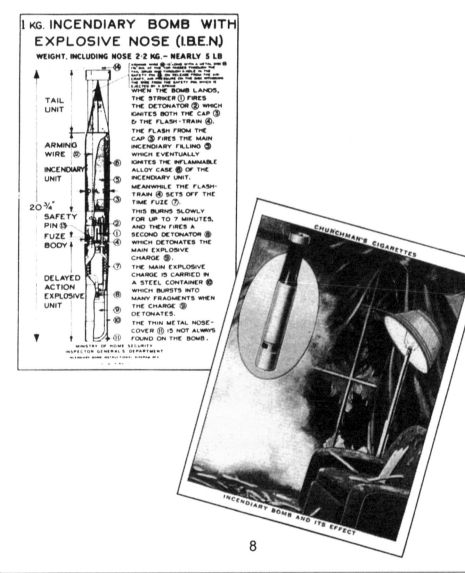

8

CHURCHMAN'S CIGARETTES

TWO-MEN PORTABLE MANUAL FIRE-PUMP IN ACTION

CHURCHMAN'S CIGARETTES

A CHAIN OF BUCKETS

CHURCHMAN'S CIGARETTES

REMOVAL OF INCENDIARY BOMB WITH SCOOP AND HOE

CHURCHMAN'S CIGARETTES

CONTROL OF INCENDIARY BOMB

CHURCHMAN'S CIGARETTES

EXTINCTION OF INCENDIARY BOMB

CHURCHMAN'S CIGARETTES

INCENDIARY BOMBS COOLING DOWN

If you had collected enough cigarette cards you knew
what to do.

9

Mother grabbed me from the bed. The night sky was
filled with lights. Searchlights, anti-aircraft fire, stars
and a bombers' moon. The sky bounced as my
mother ran. Just as we reached our dug-out across
the street, the sky flared red as the church
exploded.

It was Monday, 21 April 1941, just before 10 p.m. Thousands of incendiaries were dropped on our village, Pakefield, and the neighbouring big town, Lowestoft. The Germans were trying to set alight the thatched roof of the church to make a beacon for the following waves of bombers. Within a few minutes more than forty fires were blazing in Pakefield and the southern part of Lowestoft. Two incendiaries buried themselves in the roof of the church. The Rector climbed ladders to extinguish one, but was unable to reach the other.

The high-explosive bombs followed immediately. More were dropped in this raid than in any other, but with the church now blazing, a thick mist rolled up from the sea and ruined the bombers' night. The following waves of bombers turned back.

Summer was also the time of these: of sudden plenty, of slow hours and actions, of diamond haze and dust on the eyes, of the valley in post-vernal slumber; of burying birds out of seething corruption; of Mother sleeping heavily at noon; of jazzing wasps and dragonflies, haystooks and thistle-seeds, snows of white butterflies, skylarks' eggs, bee-orchids, and frantic ants; of wolf-cub parades, and boy scouts' bugles; of sweat running down the legs; of boiling potatoes on bramble fires, of flames glass-blue in the sun; of lying naked in the hill-cold stream; begging pennies for bottles of pop; of girls' bare arms and unripe cherries, green apples and liquid walnuts; of fights and falls and new-scabbed knees, sobbing pursuits and flights; of picnics high up in the crumbling quarries, of butter running like oil, of sunstroke, fever, and cucumber peel stuck cool to one's burning brow. All this, and the feeling that it would never end, that such days had come for ever, with the pump drying up and the water-butt crawling, and the chalk ground hard as the moon. All sights twice-brilliant and smells twice-sharp, all game-days twice as long. Double charged as we were, like the meadow ants, with the frenzy of the sun, we used up the light to its last violet drop, and even then couldn't go to bed.

When darkness fell, and the huge moon rose, we stirred to a second life. Then boys went calling along the roads, wide slit-eyed animal calls, Walt Kerry's naked nasal yodel, Boney's jackal scream. As soon as we heard them we crept outdoors, out of our stifling bedrooms, stepped out into moonlight warm as the sun to join our chalk-white, moon-masked gang.

Games in the moon. Games of pursuit and capture. Games that the night demanded. Best of all, Fox and Hounds – go where you like, and the whole of the valley to hunt through. Two chosen boys loped away through the trees and were immediately swallowed in shadow. We gave them five minutes, then set off after them. They had churchyard, farmyard, barns, quarries, hilltops, and woods to run to. They had all night, and the whole of the moon, and five miles of country to hide in....

Padding softly, we ran under the melting stars, through sharp garlic woods, through blue blazed fields, following the scent by the game's one rule, the question and answer cry. Every so often, panting for breath, we paused to check on our quarry. Bullet heads lifted, teeth shone in the moon. 'Whistle-or-'OLLER! Or-we-shall-not-FOLLER!' It was a cry on two notes, prolonged. From the other side of the hill, above white fields of mist, the faint fox-cry came back. We were off again then, through the waking night, among sleepless owls and badgers, while our quarry slipped off into another parish and would not be found for hours.

Round about midnight we ran them to earth, exhausted under a haystack. Until then we had chased them through all the world, through jungles, swamps, and tundras, across pampas plains and steppes of wheat and plateaux of shooting stars, while hares made love in the silver grasses, and the large hot moon climbed over us, raising tides in my head of night and summer that move there even yet.

War Boy

by Michael Foreman

Cider with Rosie

by Laurie Lee

A recount of past events often takes the form of an autobiography. Both the extracts you have just read fall into this category. Michael Foreman was a child during the Second World War. His book opens with a memory of one evening during wartime. In the extract from the famous autobiography based on his childhood, Laurie Lee is also recounting a memory of evening time. Although in both extracts the writers are describing events from the past, the ways in which they do so are very different.

Read, Think and Write

1. How has Michael Foreman recounted the entry of the incendiary into his house?

2. What method of dealing with the incendiary did Ivan use and how was the device finally extinguished?

3. Why were so many incendiaries dropped on to the village of Pakefield?

4. What ruined the bombers' night?

5. How does Foreman's book show what to do when an incendiary is dropped?

6. The air raid draws Michael Foreman out of doors. What draws Laurie Lee out into the evening?

7. What are the differences and similarities in the descriptions of the night sky in each extract?

8. 'Games that the night demanded.' What was the boys' favourite game, according to Laurie Lee, and what was its one rule?

9. In your own words explain how the boys described in the extract from *Cider with Rosie* played 'Fox and Hounds'.

10. Write two paragraphs to explain what an incendiary is and how it works.

Hint
Use the illustrated parts of the *War Boy* extract.

Read and Analyse

1. In the opening of the extract from *Cider with Rosie*, Laurie Lee has not written about one particular event but has given a general impression of summer. The passage is very descriptive. He has mixed together impressions of nature and the countryside with his memories of human activity.

Write down two headings: 'Nature and Countryside' and 'Human Activity'. List the various impressions from the extract under the correct heading. Has he focused on one area or is there a balanced view between the two categories in his description?

2. Spend five minutes 'brainstorming' memories of your childhood. Write down short sentences or phrases to record your impressions.

When you have completed your list of impressions, use them as the basis for a short extract from your 'autobiography'. Either choose one of them and write in the style used in *War Boy* or take several impressions and write in the more descriptive style of *Cider with Rosie*.

Hint

Think about happy or sad moments, sensations of smell, taste, colour, places, memories of people you liked or disliked, an important event.

Rather than use the title *My Life* or *My Autobiography*, both Michael Foreman and Laurie Lee use more imaginative titles for their autobiographical writing. Investigate and find other autobiography titles. What title would you use for your autobiography?

Read, Discuss and Act

1. 'all game-days twice as long … we used up the light to its last violet drop, and even then couldn't go to bed.'

Summer games were obviously very physical outdoor activities for Laurie Lee. What games do you remember playing when you were younger? Do you think children learn anything from playing games? What difference do you think computer games and Game Boys have made to children's activities?

2. With a partner prepare and give a short talk on playing games. Decide on the main point you wish to make in your talk: for example, you might want to say that games help people relax. Then use descriptions and explanations of games to back up your main point. You could include an explanation of a game you have designed yourselves.

21. In the morning we were troubled to hear it rain as it did, because of the great show tomorrow. After I was ready, I walked to my father's. And there find the late mayde to be gone and another come by my mother's choice, which my father doth not like; and so, great difference there will be between my father and mother about it. Here dined Dr. Tho. Pepys and Dr. Fayrebrother. And all our talk about tomorrow's Shewe – and our trouble that it is like to be a wet day.

After dinner comes in my Cozen Snow and his wife, and I think [to] stay there till the Shewe be*[a]* over. Then I went home; and all the way is so thronged with people to see the Triumphall Arches that I could hardly pass for them.

So home, people being at church; and I got home unseen. And, so up to my chamber and set*[b]* down these last five or six days' Diarys.

My mind a little troubled about my workmen, which being foraigners[1] are like to be troubled by a couple of lazy rogues that worked with me the other day that are Citizens: and so my work will be hindered, but I must prevent it if I can.

22.*[c]* King's going from the Tower to White-hall[2]

Up earely and made myself as fine as I could, and put on my velvet coat, the first day that I put it on though made half a year ago:[3] and being ready, Sir W. Batten, my Lady, and his two daughters and his son and wife, and Sir W. Penn and his son and I went to Mr. Young's the Flagg-maker in Cornhill;[4] and there we had a good room to ourselfs, with wine and good cake, and saw the Shew very well – in which it is impossible to relate the glory of that this day – expressed in the clothes of them that rid – and their horses and horse-cloths. Among others, my Lord Sandwich.

---

a repl.? 'being' *b* MS. 'see' *c* figure (blotted) repl. '21'

---

1. Men not enrolled as freemen of the city, though quite possibly living within its bounds. Freemen could properly object to their employment as skilled workmen within the city. (R).
2. The secular procession or royal entry held on the day before the coronation; omitted at the beginning of Charles I's reign because of the plague, and now of special magnificence because of the Restoration; never repeated after this occasion. Pepys kept in his library Hollar's prints of the cavalcade: PL 2973, pp. 340–I. For accounts both of this and of the coronation itself, see Sir Edward Walker, *Circumstantial account of the … coronation of … Charles II* (1820); John Ogilby, *The relation of his Majesties entertainment …* (1661); Evelyn, s.d.; L.G. Wickham Legg (ed.), *Engl. Coronation records*, pp 276+; *Kingd. Intell.*, 29 April; W. Kennett, *Register* (1728), pp. 411+; Rugge, I, ff. 189+
3. Above, i.227
4. Near to John Young's house, by the Royal Exchange, was the principal arch dedicated to the navy: Ogilby, p.12.

THE DIARY OF SAMUEL PEPYS

Imbroidery[1] and diamonds were ordinary among them.

The Knights of the Bath[2] was a brave sight of itself. And their Esquires, among which Mr. Armiger[3] was an Esquire to one of the Knights. remarquable was the two men that represent[a] the two Dukes of Normandy and Aquitane.[4]

The Bishops came next after the Barons, which is the higher place; which makes me think that the next parliament they will be called to the House of Lords.[5] My Lord Monke rode bare after the King, and led in his hand a spare horse, as being Maister of the Horse.

The King, in a most rich imbrodered suit and cloak, looked most nobly. Wadlow,[6] the vintner at the Devil in Fleetstreet, did lead a fine company of Souldiers, all young comely men, in white doublets. There fallowed the Vice-Chamberlin, Sir G. Carteret, a company of men all like turkes; but I know not yet what they are for.[7]

The Streets all gravelled; and the houses, hung with Carpets before them, made brave show, and the ladies out of the windows. One of which, over against us, I took much notice of and spoke of her, which made good sport among us.

So glorious was the show with gold and silver, that we were not able to look at[b] it – our eyes at last being so much overcome with it.

Both the King and the Duke of Yorke took notice of us as he saw us at the window.

The show being ended, Mr Young did give us dinner – at which we very merry, and pleased above imagination at what we have seen. <Sir W. Batten going home, he and I called and drank some Mum and laid our wager about my Lady Faulconbrige's name, which he says not to be Mary;[8] and so I won abouve 20s.>[c]

---

a repl. 'resemble'   b MS. 'up'   c addition crowded into end of line

---

1. Probably gold- and silver-thread work, with jewels.
2. 'In Crimson robes exceeding rich, & the noblest shew of the whole Cavalcade (his Majestie Excepted)': Evelyn, 23 April.
3. Probably William Armiger, a distant relative of Pepys, lodging at the house of Tom Pepys, the tailor.
4. 'In fantastique habits of that time' (Evelyn), personifying the royal claim to these duchies.
5. A bill restoring bishops to the Lords received royal assent in the following July. But they took no part in this secular cavalcade. Pepys may have been copying here from a broadsheet programme of the event (R. Williams, A true copie …, 1661) which makes the same error: E.Halfpenny in Guildhall Misc., i.no. /1021 & n.II.
6. A captain of militia.
7. They appear to have been a company of the royal footguard.
8. She was in fact Mary, daughter of Oliver Cromwell, who had married Thomas Belasyse, 2nd Viscount Fauconberg; Batten had probably confused one of her three sisters with her.

23. I lay with with Mr. Shepley, and in about 4 in the morning I rose.

Coronacion day.

And got to the abby, where I fallowed Sir J. Denham the surveyour[1] with some company that he was leading in. And with much ado, by the favour of Mr. Cooper[2] his man, did get up into a great scaffold across the north end of the abby – where with a great deal of patience I sat from past 4 till 11 before the King came in. And a pleasure it was to see the Abbey raised in the middle, all covered with red and a throne (that is a chaire) and footstoole on the top of it. And all the officers of all kinds, so much as the very fidlers, in red vests.

At last comes in the Deane and prebends of Westminster with the Bishops (many of them in cloth-of-gold Copes); and after them the nobility all in their parliament-robes, which was a most magnificent sight. Then the Duke and the King with a scepter (carried by my Lord of Sandwich) and Sword and mond before him, and the crowne too.[3]

The King in his robes, bare-headed, which was very fine. And after all had placed themselves – there was a sermon and the service. And then in the Quire at the high altar he passed all the ceremonies of the Coronacion – which, to my very great grief, I and most in the Abbey could not see. The crowne being put upon his head, a great shout begun. And he came forth to the Throne and there passed more ceremonies: as, taking the oath and having things read to him by the Bishopp,[4] and his lords (who put on their capps[5] as soon as the King put on his Crowne) and Bishopps came and kneeled before him.

And three times the King-at-armes[6] went to the three open places on the scaffold and proclaimed that if any one could show any reason why Ch. Steward should not be King of England, that now he should come and speak.

And a Generall pardon also was read by the Lord Chancellor;[7] and meddalls flung up and down by my Lord Cornwallis – of silver;[8] but I could not come by any.

---

1. Sir John Denham (poet, courtier and lettante architect) had been Surveyor-General of the King's Works since June 1660.
2. Henry Cooper, Clerk of the Works, Hampton Court.
3. The regalia, sold or destroyed in 1649, had been replaced since the Restoration by Sandwich, as Master of the Great Wardrobe, and Sir Gilbert Talbot, Master of the Jewel House. Description in Sir E. Walker, *Circumstantial Account* (1820), pp. 30+.
4. Gilbert Sheldon, Bishop of London, conducted the greater part of the service, the Archbishop of Canterbury (Juxon) being old and ill.
5. For caps and coronets, see L. G. Wickham Legg (ed.), *Engl. Coronation records*, pp. lxxxii+.
6. Sir Edward Walker, Garter King of Arms.
7. Steele, no. 3299.
8. For these coronations badges, see E. Hawkins *et al.*, *Medallic illust. hist.* G.B., i. 472–7, nos 76–85; ib., portfolio, pl. 45. Cornwallis was Treasurer of the Household.

But so great a noise, that I could make but little of the Musique; and endeed, it was lost to everybody. But I had so great a list to pisse, that I went out a little while before the King had done all his ceremonies[a] and went round the abby to Westminster-hall, all the way within rayles, and 10000 people, with the ground covered with blue cloth – and Scaffolds all the way. Into the hall I got – where it was very fine with hangings and scaffolds, one upon another, full of brave ladies. And my wife in one little one on the right hand.

Here I stayed walking up and down; and at last, upon one of the side-stalls, I stood and saw the King come in with all the persons (but the Souldiers) that were yesterday in the cavalcade;[b] and a most pleasant sight it was to see them in their several robes. And the King came in with his Crowne on and his sceptre in his hand – under a Canopy borne up by six silver staves, carried by Barons of the Cinqueports – and little bells at every end.

And after a long time he got up to the farther end, and all set themselves down at their several tables – and that was also a rare sight. And the King's first Course carried up by the Knights of the bath. And many fine ceremonies there was of the Heralds leading up people before him and bowing; and my Lord of Albimarles going to the Kitchin and eat a bit of the first dish that was to go to the King's table.[1]

But above all was these three Lords, Northumberland and Suffolke and the Duke of Ormond,[2] coming before the Courses on horseback and staying so all dinner-time; and at last, to bring up (Dymock) the King's Champion, all in armour on horseback, with his Speare and targett carried before him. And a herald[3] proclaim that if any dare deny Ch. Steward to be lawful King of England, here was a Champion that would fight with him; and with those words the Champion flings down his gantlet; and all this he doth three times in his going up toward the King's table. At last, when he is come, the King Drinkes to him and then sends him the Cup, which is of gold; and he drinks it off and then rides back again with the cup in his hand.

a repl. 'ceremonies' (blotted)   b repl. 'progress'

1. For the custom of 'assaying' royal food, see S. Pegge, *Curialia* (1791), pt iii. 30–2; cf. below, viii. 428 & n. I.
2. Lord High Constable, Earl Marshal and Lord High Steward respectively.
3. George Owen, York Herald. Pepys gives only a summary of the words used.

Day 33 – 27 October

The *Susak* seems more firmly attached to the Madras dockside than my badge to the door, for sunrise comes and we've still not moved. Nigel was up and out with the camera at a quarter to six, and an hour later, feeling rather guilty, I grab hold of the clockwork handbag, as Ron calls his tape recorder, and go out on deck to help him.

7.15 a.m.: We finally set sail. Striking juxtaposition of thin wiry, almost black Tamil stevedores, unlooping the ropes and huge, blond Schwarzeneggerian Slavs hauling them in.

So I sail away from the Coromandel Coast of India, in a Yugoslav ship, owned by a German company and registered in Cyprus. It's a Thursday morning, the delays in India have put me ten days behind Fogg's schedule, and unlike him I have no Indian princesses to show for it – only Nigel, who is not as far as I know of royal stock, and thirty pieces of BBC film equipment under my hospital bed.

The only ray of hope is that Fogg sailed from Calcutta, away to the north, so we should catch up a day or two by Singapore. Not that the *Susak* is a fast ship. Though only launched eighteen months ago at the May 3rd Shipyard in Rijeka, she is making a mere 13 knots, slower than any ship I've been on so far, with the exception of the dhow. Doubtless there are sound commercial reasons for this fuel economy, but it's frustrating for the circumnavigator.

Breakfast is at 7.30. We are served it in the officers' mess (there is strict dining and accommodation segregation between officers and crew) beneath a photo of Marshal Tito, which emphasises his spectacles so strikingly that he looks like an optician's model. The various officers come in at various times and the food, cooked by Nino, is served by Szemy. The crew divide neatly into physical types. Either they're tall, blond and cleanshaven or short, dark and bearded. The short, dark and bearded ones are the most jolly and whereas Nino has a twinkle in his eye, and has indicated that I can come into the galley for a snack any time, Szemy (best pronounced like the Glaswegian 'Jimmee') seems not altogether pleased about our presence. Breakfast consists of two fried eggs on a bed of greasy luncheon meat (which I wolf down), thick slices of Nino's home-baked white bread with butter and jam, washed down with strong Turkish coffee.

It's hard to conceive of what sort of life it must be for Yugoslavs ferrying goods they hardly ever see between three Asian cities they know nothing about, and two of which – Calcutta and Madras – they clearly dislike. This fifteen-day round trip will be their lot until May next year. The young radio officer has already had enough and will be transferred back home in January.

The *Susak* is, at 4000 tonnes, classed as a feeder ship, distributing containers, off-loaded from the big carriers, to secondary ports. It has a capacity of 330 containers and is carrying about 300 at present. Many of them seem to contain onions, and to prevent them rotting these have their doors kept open during the voyage, so a gentle shallotty aroma accompanies any walk on deck. The captain claims to have a computer print-out of all the contents of the containers, but is vague as to what their cargo might be.

'Cotton fabrics … leather … some dangerous cargo.' These are the ones with skull and crossbone markings and the word 'hazardous' stamped on the side.

We have one and a half thousand miles to go to Singapore. The sea is calm, the sky clear and sunny.

Lunch on board the Susak is at 11.30, and supper at 5.30, which takes a bit of getting used to, but it's all based around changing watches.

The cuisine is relentlessly carnivorous, and comes as a complete contrast to the delicate vegetarianism of southern India. The tea and fruit juices of India and Arabia have only limited appeal on the *Susak*, which amongst its cargo has 3000 cans of Zlatorog Export, a high quality Yugoslav lager which sports a cheery looking mountain ram as its trademark and is available at most times of day, as of course is Ballantine's Scotch, a bottle of which seems to be in every cabin, storage locker and maintenance room. With some of the meals, according to Jimmee's mood, there is Yugoslav wine, bearing the government name Vinoplod.

Much of the talk at the meal centres around shopping. Where did you get your watch? Did you know that you could get seventeen track, triple re-wind simultaneous play-back Dolby stereo music centres for 43 dollars in Singapore?

I find a place in the sun after lunch and lie on an unvisited deck, high up beside the smokestack and listen to Billy Joel and Leonard Cohen on my Walkman and read the excellent *Travellers* by Ruth Prawer Jhabwala, which tells me a lot about India, a country which it's not easy to put out of mind.

At half-past five an intense golden sun sinks beneath the horizon drawing with it all the light from the sky, which changes from off-pink to lemon to light eggshell to murky grey. The long evening, which stretches from 6.15, or earlier if Jimmee is being brisk, is devoted to Zlatorog, Vinoplod and backgammon lessons from Nigel.

Day 34 – 28 October
The clocks have gone on by one and a half hours, so sleep later. Nigel and I try our most technically ambitious adventure this morning – an interview with the captain on the bridge. This necessitates me holding the tape recorder and mike (and remembering to keep both out of shot) whilst checking the level on the recorder and answering questions. The captain has chosen this moment to give long, discursive replies and my arm is practically breaking by the end.

Finish *Travellers*, a gentle, sensitive, sensuous tale, which has restored my faith in writing. Now embark on Anthony Burgess (*Little Wilson and Big God*) and a book on Islam, about which I know woefully little. On the *Susak* mental exercise is not as problematical as physical exercise. There is nowhere to run off the effects of the Zlatorog.

The sea and weather conditions become the main source of interest. There are no other ships to be seen, only a squall of rain and a sensationally prolonged sunset, during which the surface of the Bay of Bengal seems molten.

Spend an hour or so at the prow, screened by the containers from the noise of the engine, just gazing out over the glassy silent surface of the sea, and looking down at the wash from the bows which is filled with phosphorescent pin-pricks of light. I am taking a last walk around the ship when a door opens, at the stern, letting out a long strip of light, into which a huge bull-shouldered deckhand steps, lifts his arm and sends a bottle of Ballantine's arcing high into the ocean.

The Diary of Samuel Pepys, Volume II, 1661
Around the World in 80 Days

by Michael Palin

As well as recording the events of the day, a diary may also give an account of a person's feelings and the people he or she has met. Samuel Pepys' diary has become a very useful historical document because it gives his view of events which happened over three hundred years ago.

Michael Palin has used the diary form to recount the story of, and the story behind, the making of a television series in 1988. Palin set out to circumnavigate the world, following the same route taken by Phileas Fogg 115 years earlier in Jules Vernes' book. Using trains and boats, it was a challenge to travel round the world in the time allowed. The extract is taken from the stage of their journey when they are on a very slow boat and already behind their time schedule.

Read, Think and Write

1. What do we learn about how Pepys was feeling on April 21st?

2. What events does he make a note of in his diary entry for April 21st?

3. Who does he meet on April 21st?

4. How do we know that April 22nd is an important day for Pepys? How does his writing show his excitement about the events he expects to witness?

5. What details does he give of the main event or 'Shewe' and who are the people he shares the day with?

6. Using the details from Pepys' diary entry for April 23rd, write an account of the coronation in your own words.

7. According to his account in *Around the World in 80 Days*, how is Michael Palin feeling about the journey on October 27th?

8. What details does he give of the people he shares the day with?

9. What is the main source of interest on October 28th and how is it described?

10. Write the entries the captain of the *Susak* would have needed to make in his log book for October 27th and 28th.

11. Food is a feature in this extract. Make a note of all the references you can find to food and drink.

Hint
Organise your notes under headings: 'Meal times', 'Non-mealtimes', 'Food', 'Drink'.

Read and Analyse

1. Pepys was writing in 1661. Since then there have been changes in both spelling and style of writing in the English language. Write down the following words from the extract as you would find them in a modern dictionary and give a definition and word class for each one.
   (a) imbroidery
   (b) fallowed
   (c) foraigners
   (d) remarquable
   (e) souldiers
   (f) surveyour

2. Write the entries you might find in the log book of a sailing ship for a voyage in 1661. Use the following ideas to help structure your entries:
   • an early morning embarkation
   • an evening docking three days later to take on water
   • sighting of a ship in distress
   • storm difficulties
   • crew problems
   • arrival at destination

Hint
Remember the time period.
Look at Pepys' style of writing.

Read, Discuss and Act

1. Samuel Pepys was very excited about the coronation. It was obviously a grand occasion. This country still has a monarchy and royal events are still held. Do you think royal occasions should continue? Do you think there should be another coronation in the future?

2. Michael Palin's journey was a race against time.
   In a small group, role-play a hot-air balloon journey.
   What sort of characters are in the balloon?
   Why have they come? Is it a race or a challenge,
   or perhaps a surprise birthday treat?
   Is everybody comfortable with the
   idea of being in the balloon?

Roald Dahl

Almost seventy years after the deaths of Astri and Harald, one of Roald Dahl's daughters, Tessa, wrote about her state of mind when in her own childhood comparable tragedies struck the family yet again. She described the conflict between on the one hand, feeling required to give unobtrusive support and on the other, wanting to do something extraordinary so as to be noticed amidst all the emotional drama. Above all, she longed to restore everyone's happiness. Dahl rarely talked about his own feelings, but he must have had to cope with all this when he was only four years old – this, and the additional pride and burden of being his mother's only son. Only child was what it seems to have felt like, despite – or perhaps partly because of – the size of the family. His nickname at home was 'the Apple' because he was the apple of his mother's eye. It was an ambiguous role – privileged but demanding. Much was expected of him and although he never lacked either encouragement or material rewards, his mother showed him little physical warmth. The bereaved boy was both the centre of attention and very lonely.

It is as lone operators that children were to figure in his stories. Matilda, in the book named after her, has a negligible brother, but otherwise all Dahl's main child characters are without siblings. Many of the stories are centred on orphans: 'Katina', 'Pig', *James and the Giant Peach*, *The BFG*, *The Witches*. Others, such as *Danny the Champion of the World*, involve an intense relationship between a single child and a single parent or surrogate parent. It is, of course, a classic situation in children's literature – partly because writers are often people who have felt isolated as children. But when, late in his life, Dahl was asked by a television interviewer about this emphasis in his work, he seemed surprised and at first denied that it existed.

Sofie, Dahl was to write, 'was undoubtedly the absolute primary influence on my own life. She had a crystal-clear intellect and a deep interest in almost everything under the sun… She was the matriarch, the materfamilias, and her children radiated round her like planets round a sun.' He explored the relationship in 'Only This', a story about a bomber pilot and his mother which he wrote in Washington in the 1940s. The emotional centre is not the man's feelings, but the woman's for him. She is seen through the bedroom window of a moonlit English cottage. Awakened by bombers flying overhead to Germany, she sits up thinking about her only son, who is flying in one of them. In her thoughts she flies with him. He hears her speak to him and touches her shoulder before the aircraft is hit by flak and crashes. Son and mother both die, he in the cockpit, she at her bedroom window. The title refers to a passage early in the story where Dahl describes both the mother's feelings for her child and, by implication, his for her: 'the deep conscious knowing that there was nothing else to live for except this.'

In its intensity, 'Only This' may have been touched not only by Dahl's direct feelings as a son and a pilot, but by something he had read when he was still at prep school and which, he later said, 'profoundly fascinated and probably influenced' him. *Can Such Things Be*, a collection of the *fin-de-siècle* US writer Ambrose Bierce, begins with a sinister, psychologically turbulent episode, 'The Death of Halpin Frayser'. A young man, neglected by his powerful father, spoilt by his mother, 'of a dreamy, indolent and rather romantic turn, somewhat … addicted to literature', decides to leave home for California. His mother does all she can to stop him, but even when she describes a dream of her own death, he is unpersuaded. Having gone, he is prevented from returning. Shanghaied in San Francisco and shipwrecked in the South Pacific, he is kept away for six years. On his way back at last, Frayser dreams that his mother has been murdered. His guilty fantasy – with which the intricately-structured narrative opens – turns out to be true. Widowed, and unsuccessful in her search for her lost son, his mother remarried. The new husband killed her. …

The young Roald was so taken with Bierce's book that he gave it to his best friend at prep school, Douglas Highton, whose parents lived apart and whose own home was also with his mother. Many years later Dahl asked for it back, and Highton exchanged it for signed copies of Dahl's own books.

The two boys were boarders at St Peter's School, Weston-super-Mare. However, it was not until 1925 that Sofie sent her son there. Her first action after Harald's death was to buy a double-fronted, red-brick Victorian house in Cardiff Road, Llandaff, close to where Harald's business partner lived, and close, too, to a new school for girls and small boys. Alfhild, Else, Roald and Asta all in turn went to Elm Tree House, which was then in Ely Road, near the fields, with a well-stocked garden behind. In the summer, lessons were held among the much-raided fruit bushes. Miss Tucker, one of the two sisters who ran the school, taught nature study.

Dahl often referred to his childhood fascination with birds, moles, butterflies, gnats. He vividly recalled experiments such as eating the bulb of a buttercup ('frighteningly hot') or putting an ear of barley under his sleeve and feeling it climb to his shoulder. Some of this fascination came, he liked to think, from Sofie's prenatal 'glorious walks', but it may also have been influenced by her father. Certainly, it was nourished on the family's annual Norwegian holidays. Although none of them would ever live in Norway, Harald and Sofie's children were brought up with a strong sense of belonging there. They were christened in the Norwegian church in Cardiff docks. They learned to speak Norwegian. Every summer, Sofie took them home to join her overwhelmingly female tribe, where they ate fresh fish and burnt toffee, and heard stories of trolls and witches. The family included both good cooks and good story-tellers.

It would be hard to miss the influence of northern European folk-tales on Dahl's stories. Witches, and 'hags' in general, took a particular hold. Not that in the 1920s you had to be Scandinavian, or a boy brought up in a matriarchy, to be scared of witches – particularly in druidical Wales. The small boy was especially horrified by an old woman who ran a sweet shop in Llandaff, 'a small skinny old hag with a moustache on her upper lip and a mouth as sour as a green gooseberry.' Four chapters of *Boy* are given over to an episode in which Roald and his friends put a dead mouse in one of her jars and are repaid with a caning. In its comic extravagance, much of *Boy* reads like fiction, but Dahl wasn't the only Llandaff child to have kept such memories. His contemporary, Mrs Ferris, who went to the local primary school which then stood opposite the sweet shop, vividly recalls its proprietors. 'Two sisters, weren't they? Very old, oh, very decrepit. We didn't like going in there, you see ... We used to be a bit frightened, because they were like witches, weren't they?'

One's mother apart, any woman might be a witch in the sub-culture in which Dahl was soon to be enrolled. It had always been Harald Dahl's intention to send his children to English 'public' schools, and his widow was sure that Roald needed the influence of men. If he was to get into public school, he would have to be prepared for the Common Entrance exam. He was moved briefly from Elm Tree House to the Cathedral School on the green in Llandaff. There he was a day-boy, but at the age of nine he arrived with his trunk in the long corridors of St Peter's Preparatory School, Weston-super-Mare. You can just see the town from Cardiff docks, on the muddy far bank of the Severn.

Extinct today, St Peter's had been founded in 1900. It was unusual in having been purpose-built as a prep school: a long building from whose spinal corridor branched six classrooms, above which were six dormitories each housing a dozen boys. At one end of the building, in a part strictly out of bounds to them, lived the headmaster, his wife and their two daughters. These girls were objects of fascination not much calmed by their father's pedagogical approach to the Facts of Life.

In later life, Roald Dahl would describe his sex education in a comic set piece with which he regaled family parties, booksellers' conferences and publishers' gatherings, and even the Prize Days of schools. According to one who heard it, it went roughly like this. The headmaster told the boys, 'You have about your body a certain organ. I think you know what I'm talking about.' (Dahl would say, 'And I think we did know what he was talking about.') 'Well, I want you to realize that it's like a torch. There's a sort of bulb on the end of it. It you touch it, it will light up. And if it lights up, your batteries will go flat.' That was all. Except that afterwards, according to the story, Roald didn't dare touch his penis. Even drying himself after a bath was a source of anxiety, until one holiday when a sister acquired a hair dryer and his problem was solved.

St Peter's itself, if we are to believe Dahl's description in *Boy*, was a cross between Dotheboys Hall and Llanabba Castle, the gothic prep school of Evelyn Waugh's *Decline and Fall*. Waugh's louche master, Captain Grimes, in particular has his Dahl counterpart in 'Victor' Corrado, in love with the sadistic school matron. Dahl had to concede to his St Peter's friend Highton that *Boy* was 'coloured by my natural love of fantasy'; Highton himself found the school ordinary enough. He now thinks that in its attempt to instil integrity and qualities of leadership in a pack of unregenerate seven-to-thirteen-year-olds, the regime was 'a bit strict', but he remembers most of the staff – including the matron – as having been perfectly normal, capable and kind: 'None of it was as grim as in *Boy*.' But he recalls one Dahl-like streak of waywardness when a master become keen on the mother of a pupil and gave the boy an enviably large model racing car. The man later turned up under a pseudonym, seemingly as a spy, at the headquarters of a secret experimental armoured division where Highton was a security officer in the Second World War. Knowing that the background he claimed was false, Highton had him removed by MI5.

Dahl himself, to eyes other than his own, seems to have passed his four years at St Peter's unexceptionally. He was tall, soft-faced, neither especially popular nor unpopular, although very close to the few boys who became his friends. (Douglas Highton still has the presents Dahl brought him back from holidays in Norway: a model seal itself made from seal-skin; a paper-knife carved from part of a reindeer's antler; a sketchy carving of a reindeer pulling a sleigh.) Dahl's letters home, meanwhile, were routinely full of football and stamp collecting, Bonfire Night fireworks and the finer points of conkers. He was good at games, promising well at cricket (the school magazine said 'we expect great things in the future') and winning prizes for swimming. Like everyone else, he marched in crocodile on Sundays to All Saints Church, Weston-super-Mare, and called it All Stinks because of the incense. Like everyone else, he made tobacco out of the Virginia creeper on the school wall and smoked it, sickeningly, in a clay pipe.

Academically he was weak: towards the bottom of his form of thirteen boys in Latin and Maths, and only slightly better at English. This must have been a blow to a child who was the centre of attention at home, and of whom, since his father's death, so much was expected. And however comprehensible, practically speaking, he found his mother's decision to send him away to school, it still bewildered and hurt him. In his first term, in an instinctively well-aimed bid for her attention, he faked the symptoms of the appendicitis from which Astri had died, and won a short reprieve. But as time went by, and as he adapted himself to the inevitable, Dahl found other escape routes. In particular, he absorbed himself in stories. He remembered any narrative he read or was told. In his earliest letters home he relates verbatim a dramatized reading from Dickens and a school lecture on bird legends – he particularly admired the 'fine' story in which the King of the Birds is whichever bird can fly highest, and the wren wins by hiding in the feathers of the eagle. As time went by, he read avidly among the novelists of exploration and military adventure popular among boys at the time: Kipling, Captain Marryat, H. Rider Haggard, G. A. Henty, writers whose emphasis on heroism and masculinity was to influence his life as well as his books.

He seems sometimes to have believed in stories more than he believed in people. If *Boy* is enjoyable for its violence – macabre episodes involving dentistry, car accidents, school beatings, the lancing of a friend's boil – the main *dramatis personae* are correspondingly worked up into caricatures. In a couple of cases Dahl thought it best to change names. In others, he simply misremembered them: Victor for Valentine, Braithwaite for Blathwayt, Wragg for Ragg. He was sixty-seven when he wrote the book and his spelling was always erratic. But it seems not to have troubled him, as he conjured these people up, that they were real and independent, not simply characters in a world of his own invention. This was to become a controversial issue because of some of the things he wrote in *Boy* about this next school.

St Peter's sent its pupils on to good, sound, middling public schools: Blundell's, Charterhouse, Cheltenham, Radley. Highton won a scholarship to Oakham. Dahl got into Repton.

A Midland village seven miles south of Derby, Repton is a dour little sprawl of blackened stone and red brick overlooking the featureless Trent valley. There is nothing much there except the school. Priory House, where Dahl was to spend the next four and a half years, appears from the outside pleasantly domestic. A tile-hung Victorian villa with a corner turret, bay windows and an enclosed garden, it could have been his old home in Llandaff. Yet inside, day and night, week in, week out, the older boys of the house were licensed to terrorize the younger. Repton was 'a tough place', one Priory contemporary recalls: 'Rules and discipline tight, living really spartan, enforced by boys who did 90 per cent of the beating, of which there was a lot'.

The family had recently moved close to London, to a comfortable eight-bedroomed house in Bexley, Kent, more convenient for trains to the school attended by all of Dahl's sisters, Roedean in Sussex. The new family home was called Oakwood. With its tennis court, its table-tennis table in the conservatory and the huge breakfasts ready in the dining room on little flame heaters, it could not have contrasted more sharply with the rigours of school.

Repton, according to another of Dahl's contemporaries, the philosopher Sir Stuart Hampshire, had 'all the worst features of Marlborough or Eton without any of the sophistication. It was full of heavy plutocratic boys from the North.' Not so full though that it didn't find room at the same time for the future novelist Denton Welch. It is the fate of all schools that some of their liveliest pupils grow up to revile them. Repton has been unluckier in this respect than most. Welch's classic autobiography, *Maiden Voyage*, begins with his attempt not to return to the school in the autumn of 1931 (when Dahl had been there for five terms). Much of what Welch ran away from corresponds with Dahl's account in *Boy*: fagging, beatings, the torture of new boys and other miseries common to many, although not all, boys' boarding schools of the time. There are other, more pleasant memories, including some peculiar to Repton – such as the market research done there by Cadbury's and described in *Boy*. A plain cardboard box full of new types of chocolate was given to every boy, with a check-list on which he had to award marks to each. Dahl's taste for high-street brands of chocolate was already well established. The Cadbury's blind tastings turned it into a lifelong addiction.

Roald Dahl

by Jeremy Treglown

It is an interesting, though sometimes difficult, task to recount someone's life, but that is just the task a biographer sets themselves. The biographer must research their subject very carefully before starting to write. Jeremy Treglown chose to write about a very well-known author: in fact, it is probably nearly impossible for anyone to go through childhood without reading a Roald Dahl book!

Many biographies follow the sequence of the person's life, so you will often find that the beginning of the book deals with the subject's childhood. The extract on the previous pages is taken from the second chapter, entitled 'The Apple'. The author has just recounted the death of Dahl's father, Harald, and how this left his mother to bring up the family.

Read, Think and Write

1. Why was Roald Dahl given the nickname 'the Apple'?

2. What does the author point out about many of Roald Dahl's stories, such as *James and the Giant Peach*, *The BFG* and *The Witches*? Does he think Roald Dahl would have agreed with him?

3. What details are given of Roald Dahl's Norwegian background?

4. After he left the Cathedral School in Llandaff, Roald Dahl went to St Peter's Preparatory School. How does the writer describe this school?

5. The writer balances Roald Dahl's view of St Peter's given in *Boy* with the view of Dahl's friend Douglas Highton. What are the differences and similarities in the two points of view?

6. Roald Dahl wrote letters home while at St Peter's. What do we learn about his interests and school life from those letters?

7. After leaving St Peter's, Roald Dahl went to Repton. How does the writer describe this school?

8. Many of Roald Dahl's memories of Repton are of unpleasant events. What pleasant memory does he recount in his autobiography, *Boy*?

9. According to Dahl, Sofie, his mother, 'was undoubtedly the absolute primary influence on my own life'. How does the writer show this influence developing in what Dahl wrote and read?

10. The facts and opinions about Roald Dahl presented in this extract begin to build a picture of his character. Using evidence from the text to show his interests, his likes and dislikes, his fears and the influences on him, write a short character study of Roald Dahl.

Read and Analyse

1. A recount of events involves a point of view. In a biography, facts may be placed alongside opinion. Write down five facts and five opinions from the extract.

2. Look at six paragraphs in the extract starting 'One's mother apart, any woman …' and ending '… was to influence his life as well as his books'.

Hint
Look at use of punctuation and position of subordinate phrases and clauses..

Rewrite the opening sentence of each paragraph in this section without changing its meaning.

3. Write the following extracts from the text in your own words.
   (a) 'intricately-structured narrative'
   (b) 'vividly recalls its proprietors'
   (c) 'a controversial issue'
   (d) 'an ambiguous role – privileged but demanding'

Read, Discuss and Act

1. According to Jeremy Treglown's biography, Roald Dahl's mother had a great influence on him. How much influence do you think parents have or should have on their children?

2. Biographies tend to be written about famous people. Would there be any value in writing a biography of an ordinary person? If you were asked to write a biography of someone, who would you choose and why?

3. In a small group, use the extract to prepare and act a scene from the television programme 'This is Your Life'. The presenter could introduce and talk with Roald Dahl and then bring on his friend Douglas Highton, who would add his memories to the discussion.

Develop the idea further by role-playing how you think other famous characters from the past might be presented on the programme.

How it all started

1889

1904-5

2002 will be a very special year for the Reds, because it will be the 100th year of Manchester United. The club first played under that name on 6 September 1902, but what were they called before then? And how did the first team get together? For answers to these questions, and a few others, read on …

On the right track

The first 'United' players were actually workers in the Carriage and Wagon department of the Lancashire and Yorkshire Railway. They formed a football team in 1878, calling themselves Newton Heath LYR and playing on a pitch in North Road, near to their railway yard.

Local heroes

Newton Heath proved they were a good team when they entered the Manchester Cup, a competition for all football clubs in the city and the surrounding area. They won the Cup in 1886, and finished as runners-up in 1885 and 1887. The railway bosses were so impressed, they gave the players time off to train!

Time for a new challenge

Bored with local football and friendlies, the Heathens entered the national Football League in 1892. Robert Donaldson scored their first league goal but they still lost their first game, 4–3 at Blackburn. The club didn't win until their seventh match, when Donaldson scored a hat-trick in the 10–1 thrashing of Wolves!

Moving home

The Heathens hoped that moving to a new ground at Bank Street, Clayton, would bring them better luck. Sadly the air was polluted by factory fumes, and the pitch had more sand on it than grass. When Walsall played there, they complained so much that their 14–1 defeat was later wiped from the records!

Dog to the rescue

Struggling for money in the Second Division, Newton Heath decided to hold a fund-raising fair that opened on 27 February 1901. The club struck lucky when the St Bernard dog belonging to captain Harry Stafford escaped from the show and was found by the wealthy owner of a local brewery, John Henry Davies …

New money, new name

Mr Davies and Mr Stafford saved the club in 1902 when Newton Heath went bankrupt. Davies became club president, while a man called Louis Rocca suggested a new name – Manchester United. The new team won their first match, against Gainsborough Trinity, won the League in 1908, the FA Cup in 1909 and moved to Old Trafford in 1910. **So now you know!**

A long, long time ago … this is how the United teams and Old Trafford itself used to look.

1892-3

45

From dietician to doctor, kit man to masseur, the film introduced us to some of the men in **Sir Alex Ferguson's secret army**, a special collection of men often known as the backroom boys. You might recognise some of the faces, but do you know their names? And what are their roles and responsibilities inside the Red machine? Read on...

Steve McClaren
He was perhaps the most famous face in Sir Alex Ferguson's support team for three seasons; in fact, some people thought he would be great as the next manager of United. As a player, Steve didn't exactly perform at the highest level (sorry, Hull, Oxford and co.) but as an **assistant manager**, he worked in the Premiership with Derby County before helping United win the Treble in his first half-season! He even coached the England national team for a few games during 2000/01.

One of his favourite training routines at Carrington was an exercise in which the lads had to sprint to either the left or the right, depending on his shout. At the same time, he would often point in completely the opposite direction, just to catch them out. The United players thought very highly of Steve and were sorry to see him leave for Middlesbrough in June 2001.

Jimmy Ryan
Unlike Steve, Jimmy did play at the highest level, for Manchester United! If you ever see a team photo from 1968, when the Reds first won the European Cup, you might spot him in the line-up. He was a tricky winger way back then, and he can still turn on the skill in training. Just ask Beckham, Butt, Giggs, Scholes and the Nevilles; Jim worked with them all during his time in charge of United Reserves from 1991 to 1999, and he's now training them again, as **first team coach**. In fact, while Fergie was away, he was even the manager for a day in December 1999. Unlucky for Jim, the Reds lost the match, 3–2 to Middlesbrough.

Tony Coton
TC also played for the Reds, but only in the Reserves while acting as cover for Peter Schmeichel in 1996. In fact, he was better known as a goalkeeper on the other side of town, with Manchester City. Before his spell with the Blues, he played for Watford and Birmingham City, where he saved a penalty on his debut. Now employed as United's specialist **goalkeeping coach**, Coton has helped Paul Rachubka and Nick Culkin to come through with confidence and make appearances in the first team.

Rob Swire
As **senior physiotherapist**, Rob's role is one of the most important at the club. It's his job on a match-day to keep his eye on the United players and be ready to rush on if any of them get injured. He has first-class first-aid skills and carries a well-stocked medical bag, which is designed to deal with on-the-pitch problems very quickly and cleanly. Rob is also a busy man during the week, helping his team of physios to prepare the club's many players for action by easing their aches, pains and strains. He might even be asked to test the fitness of a potential new signing, to make sure they're in the very best condition to play for United.

Dr Mike Stone
The job of football **club doctor** used to be part-time, but now that the medical side of the game is so important, and United have so many players, Dr Stone is now a full-time member of the backroom staff. Like his close colleague Rob Swire, the Doc is based in the medical centre at Carrington but travels with the first team wherever they go. He can prescribe medicines to the players if they're feeling ill, but he has to check carefully first, to make sure the tablets or drugs are not banned from use in professional football.

Albert Morgan and Alec Wylie
Ever wondered who has the nice job of washing the shirts, shorts and socks? Well, wonder no more, because Albert (pictured) and Alec are the **kit managers** who make sure the players are well turned out in red, white or blue. Helped by a team of laundry ladies, AM and AW are responsible for the collecting, cleaning, storing, transporting and sometimes the repairing of all the kit worn by all of the club's teams. Albert and Alec also have the keys to the special room where all the players' boots are kept.

Jimmy Curran and Trevor Lea
Jimmy (pictured) is part of the medical team at Carrington and Old Trafford. He's been at the club for more years than he'd like to admit to, serving with a smile and sometimes a song in various jobs, but most recently as **assistant to the physios** and **masseur** to the stars! Meanwhile, **club dietician** Trevor Lea makes sure the players consume the food and drink they need to perform at the highest level. Boiled rice, grilled chicken, fish and pasta may seem boring and bland compared to burgers and chips, but take it from Trev, they can do the trick!

 MANCHESTER UNITED ANNUAL 2002 57

Manchester United Annual 2002

Explanatory texts are often centred on the question of how a machine is made and how it functions. The Manchester United Annual provides information about the 'Red Machine' and explanations about how it all started and how it works. The two extracts are taken from different parts of the annual. The 'Backroom Boys' feature refers to the Manchester United movie *Beyond the Promised Land* in its opening paragraph.

Read, Think and Write

1. Why is 2002 a special year for Manchester United?

2. What was the club called before it became Manchester United and who were the first players?

3. What problems did the team have at their new ground in Bank Street?

4. Draw a flow chart to show the main sequence of events in the club's history from 1878 to 1910.

5. Why is the club physiotherapist important?

6. Why must the doctor be careful when he prescribes medicine for the players?

7. How does the club dietician help the players?

8. Name two ways in which Jimmy Ryan has helped train the team.

9. Both extracts make use of headings to introduce each section of text. Replace each of the names in the 'Backroom Boys' extract with a 'tabloid'-style heading: e.g. for Steve McClaren you might have 'Point and shout to catch them out'.

10. Write a newspaper report for the game between the 'Heathens' and Walsall at the Bank Street ground when the score was 14–1.

Hint
Remember the conditions described in 'Moving home'.

Read and Analyse

1. Make a list of all the proper nouns in both extracts. Find ten common nouns from the extracts and put them into sentences of your own.

   Use a thesaurus to help you find and write down six abstract nouns to name the qualities of a good football player.

   The word 'team' is a collective noun. Write down six more examples of collective nouns.

2. Choose one of the 'Backroom Boys' and write out the passage as a question-and-answer conversation. Remember the conventions of speech.

   Example
   Jimmy Ryan
   "Did you play for Manchester United?"
   "Yes, I played for them in 1968 when the Reds first won the European Cup."

Read, Discuss and Act

1. In a small group, prepare a presentation on the subject of football. You might consider some of these questions. Why do you think football is such a high-profile sport? Do you think so much time should be given over to it on television? Do you think football supporters have a bad image? Do you think players are worth the amount of money they can earn?

   Try to put both negative and positive points of view in your presentation in order to promote discussion and questions from your audience.

2. In pairs, role-play the scene in a commentary box where two football commentators are describing loudly and enthusiastically a game in progress while they are 'on air', but chatting in a quiet and friendly manner about their recent holidays when the microphone is off. Keep switching from one discussion to the other. Do the commentators get confused by conducting two discussions at the same time?

Origins of our planet

Big Bang 16 billion years ago

Formation of galaxy

Oldest stars in galaxy formed

Billions of years ago | 15 | 14 | 13 | 12 | 11 | 10 | 9

The only life in the universe of which we have evidence began on this earth between three and four billion years ago. The conditions present on its surface at that time provided the basic ingredients—liquid water and carbon compounds—out of which all known life is constructed. But where did the earth come from? Why were the conditions appropriate for the creation of life to be found here and, so far as is known, nowhere else in the solar system?

All matter in the universe was originally formed during the early phases of the "Big Bang" that brought the universe into existence—an explosion of unimaginable violence which took place about 16 billion years ago. Beginning as a small, intensely hot entity, the universe has from that moment on been expanding and cooling. In the early stages of its expansion, it contained only subatomic particles and waves of radiation. Later, the nuclei of hydrogen atoms coalesced. Subsequently, fusion of these basic nuclei and their capture of electrons led to the creation of all the other, heavier elements.

The matter out of which the early universe was composed was not distributed evenly, however, and gravitational attraction brought about further clusterings. Such giant concentrations of gas and dust were the starting material for galaxies—island sub-universes each containing enough matter for billions of stars. In each galactic mass, individual clouds of matter were the beginnings of stars like our sun.

Birth of the solar system

Modern theories vary, but most agree that the sun did not "capture" its family of circling planets by gravitational attraction. They suggest that the entire solar system was created at the same time, between 4.5 and 5 billion years ago. The story probably began with a roughly spherical cloud of hydrogen and dust. Gravity caused this cloud to collapse toward its own centre and begin to rotate. But as it picked up speed, the shape of the giant spinning cloud began to change. It flattened out like a disc, with a spherical central bulge.

Hydrogen nuclei at the centre of bulge were squeezed by gravity reached such a high density that fusio the process that fuels the hydro bomb—began to occur. Helium nu were produced and enormous quanti of energy were given off in the form of and light. The sun had begun to shi

Elsewhere in the spinning disc, mos the swirling gas and dust particles coll and stuck together, "glued" by elec static and other forces to form ever-la "rocks". Eventually these acquired su cient mass to exercise a strong grav tional attraction, and planets were for from the aggregated matter.

The four planets that lie closest to heat of the sun—Mercury, Venus, Ea and Mars—are formed from clusters material with high melting points: all rocky, with metal cores. Farther out found the frigid gas giants, Jupiter, S urn, Uranus and Neptune.

Early on in its history, the ear substance sorted itself into layers. Hea to nearly 4,000°C by the natural decay

Mercury
Mean daytime surface
temperature: 330°C
Mean night-time surface
temperature: –180°C
Mean distance from sun:
57.9 million km
Virtually no atmosphere,
no greenhouse effect

Venus
Mean surface
temperature: 480°C
Mean distance from sun:
108.2 million km
Thick atmosphere,
containing much carbon
dioxide; strong
greenhouse effect

12

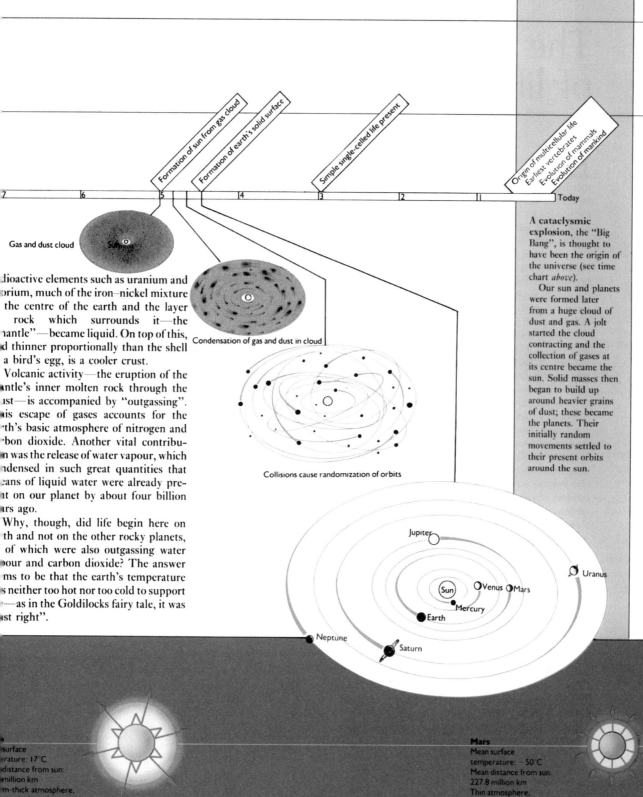

Global patterns

Formation of sun from gas cloud

Formation of earth's solid surface

Simple single-celled life present

Origin of multicellular life
Earliest vertebrates
Evolution of mammals
Evolution of mankind

7 · 6 · 5 · 4 · 3 · 2 · 1 · Today

Gas and dust cloud

Condensation of gas and dust in cloud

Collisions cause randomization of orbits

…dioactive elements such as uranium and …orium, much of the iron–nickel mixture … the centre of the earth and the layer … rock which surrounds it—the …antle"—became liquid. On top of this, …d thinner proportionally than the shell … a bird's egg, is a cooler crust.

…Volcanic activity—the eruption of the …antle's inner molten rock through the …ust—is accompanied by "outgassing". …is escape of gases accounts for the …rth's basic atmosphere of nitrogen and …rbon dioxide. Another vital contribu-…n was the release of water vapour, which …ndensed in such great quantities that …eans of liquid water were already pre-…t on our planet by about four billion …ars ago.

…Why, though, did life begin here on …th and not on the other rocky planets, … of which were also outgassing water …our and carbon dioxide? The answer …ms to be that the earth's temperature … neither too hot nor too cold to support …—as in the Goldilocks fairy tale, it was …st right".

A cataclysmic explosion, the "Big Bang", is thought to have been the origin of the universe (see time chart *above*).

Our sun and planets were formed later from a huge cloud of dust and gas. A jolt started the cloud contracting and the collection of gases at its centre became the sun. Solid masses then began to build up around heavier grains of dust; these became the planets. Their initially random movements settled to their present orbits around the sun.

Jupiter

Uranus

Sun · Venus · Mars
Mercury
Earth

Neptune

Saturn

…surface
…erature: 17°C
…distance from sun:
…million km
…m-thick atmosphere.
…ning little carbon
…e although level is
…sing; medium
…ouse effect

Mars
Mean surface
temperature: −50°C
Mean distance from sun:
227.8 million km
Thin atmosphere,
containing very little
carbon dioxide;
little greenhouse effect

13

The origins of life

Life is a comparatively fragile phenomenon, which can exist only within a narrow range of conditions. Yet in the vastness of the universe, it is assumed that the conditions necessary for the evolution of life must have occurred many times.

The earth on which life first evolved was, however, very different from the planet of today: the very oxygen that we breathe, and the protective ozone layer of the earth's atmosphere, did not exist then for they are themselves the products of that life.

The oldest direct traces of life on earth date back 3.4–3.5 billion years. In rocks that age in Australia and southern Africa geologists have found stromatolites, layered structures created through the activity of primitive algae or bacteria. Other Australian rocks of similar age provide even more direct evidence of ancient life. Sections of these rocks, known as cherts, show the fossilized remains of blue-green algae themselves.

Rocks also reveal even more distant, indirect traces of life. Living things use particular isotopes (physical forms) of the element carbon preferentially. The mix of carbon isotopes detected in rocks from Greenland more than 3.8 billion years old show evidence of life on earth—that is, only 600 million years after the planet itself was first formed.

What is life?

Reduced to its barest essentials, life is the ability of an organic substance to produce a replica of itself. In organisms alive today, that ability is found only in molecules like DNA—deoxyribonucleic acid.

The huge information-carrying molecule of DNA is similar to a set of detailed plans, and the plans are for making proteins. From proteins, whose production and packaging is controlled by the endoplasmic reticulum and Golgi bodies of plant and animal cells, DNA can build itself a cell. When the cell divides in two, each daughter cell needs a copy of the master plan for making new cells. So, before the division, the DNA copies itself so that a version of the DNA plan can be passed into each of the two newly formed cells.

In the blue-green algae, organisms with ancient origins, the DNA is found loose in an uncomplicated cell. This "prokaryote" structure is simpler than the "eukaryote" one, in which the DNA is organized into threadlike chromosomes and housed within a cell nucleus. Eukaryotes are thought to have evolved two billion years after their prokaryote ancestors.

Whether simple or complex, all living matter is made primarily of the compounds of carbon, oxygen, hydrogen and nitrogen, which would have been abundant in the earth's early atmosphere in the form of gases such as water vapour, nitrogen and carbon dioxide. Each of these gases is given off during volcanic activity, which was very frequent at that time.

If ultraviolet light or lightning act such an atmosphere, a variety of s organic compounds are formed. An form of DNA could have been made such ingredients. Once the first DN molecule had appeared, it would r have reproduced itself. Then natu lection would have come into play, fa ing the survival of those variants adapted to quick, effective reprod and vigorous offspring.

DNA replication became much effective through the evolution of th within whose walls or membran substances such as proteins. Mor amino acids, the building blocks which proteins are constructed, are taneously formed in the chemically tive conditions believed to be pres the earth's early history.

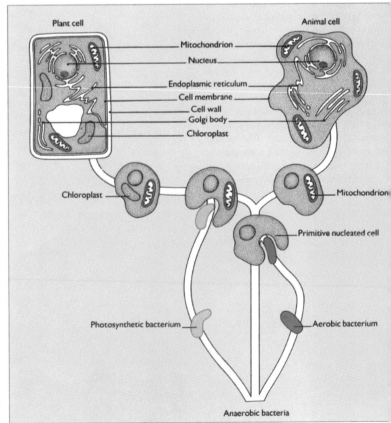

Plant cell — Animal cell
Mitochondrion
Nucleus
Endoplasmic reticulum
Cell membrane
Cell wall
Golgi body
Chloroplast
Chloroplast — Mitochondrion
Primitive nucleated cell
Photosynthetic bacterium — Aerobic bacterium
Anaerobic bacteria

Another development of immense importance was the evolution of the green pigment chlorophyll, for this allowed cells to trap sunlight and use it to produce their own energy. As a by-product of this process of photosynthesis, early plants, like their modern counterparts, released oxygen.

The oxygen produced by plants at first became "locked up" by reacting or combining with other substances and minerals. Eventually, some 2.2 billion years ago, free oxygen was present in the atmosphere. Living things used this reactive substance in the biochemical functions of their own cells. The free oxygen in the atmosphere also produced a layer of ozone, which filters out the ultraviolet light from the sun that is harmful to life below.

Complex cells (*left*) may have evolved by the permanent combination of more simple cells. If a simple anaerobic bacterium, an organism living without oxygen, engulfed an aerobic bacterium, the newcomer could have become a mitochondrion, the cell organelle that uses oxygen to provide energy. In a similar way, the chlorophyll-containing chloroplasts typical of plant cells may have originated as photosynthetic bacteria. Plant cells also differ from those of animals in having thick rigid walls.

The DNA molecule (*right*) is at the heart of all earthly life and is built like a ladder. Each "rung" is made of a pair of chemicals—either adenine and thymine or cytosine and guanine. When the molecule replicates itself, the helix unwinds and new bases are added from a "pool" available in the cell. Thus two perfect copies of the original helix are produced.

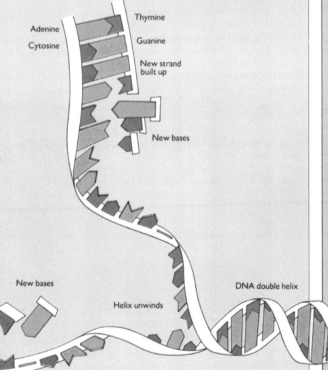

Adenine
Cytosine
Thymine
Guanine

New strand built up

New bases

New bases

New strand built up

Helix unwinds

DNA double helix

Some of the oldest evidence of life on earth, dating back about 3.5 billion years, is contained in stromatolites, rocklike structures such as these at Shark Bay, Australia.

They are formed by primitive organisms, blue-green algae. As the algae grow they form a web of material in which sediments from the surrounding water are trapped and eventually compacted into a dense mat. Another algal web then forms above this layer and this too forms a sediment mat. The process continues, gradually shaping the mound- or even pillar-like structures known as stromatolites.

17

The Atlas of the Living World

by David Attenborough

The words 'how' and 'why' usually herald an explanation. The diversity of phenomena in the world around us means that explanatory writing will be found in a wide variety of texts covering all subjects. The extracts on the previous four pages deal with what might be considered the ultimate subject for an explanation – how did it all begin?

1. How and when was all matter in the universe formed?

2. What are galaxies?

3. How did the sun begin to shine?

4. What two things contributed to the earth's basic atmosphere?

5. An explanation usually has an opening summary statement. In your own words, write down the main idea from each of the first four paragraphs of 'The origins of life'.

6. What is life when reduced to 'its barest essentials'?

7. What are the differences between a plant cell and an animal cell?

8. Why was the evolution of the green pigment chlorophyll important to all life?

9. Why was free oxygen important to the development of life?

10. Write a one-page article for a science magazine explaining what DNA is and how important it is to life.

Read and Analyse

1. Explanations often need to use technical language. Use a dictionary and the context of the extract to make a glossary of twelve technical words found in the extract.

   Example
   fusion – the act or an instance of fusing or melting

2. Using the information in the text, write a simple explanation for a young child showing how the earth and its life forms began.

Hint
Pick out the main points. Diagrams and illustrations can help to make explanations clearer.

Read, Discuss and Act

1. There is much evidence to support the 'Big Bang' theory, but it is still only a theory. Do you believe it? What other explanations are there or might there be for the origins of the universe?

2. If you look again at the timeline in the extract, you will see that the earth existed for a long time before life evolved. Is life in all its forms developed from a biochemical process? Might there be a missing element in the chemical process? The extract gives a scientific explanation for the question 'What is life?'. How else might you answer this question?

3. In a small group, role-play a situation where alien life forms from another galaxy visit and interact with human life forms. The aliens are collecting information about earth and therefore require explanations about the many phenomena they experience on earth. Naturally the human characters are very curious about the aliens' lifestyle and also want explanations.

How to make your own coal...

1. You will need one giant horsetail – say 40 metres (140 feet) in height.

2. Cut down the horsetail and allow it to rot in warm smelly water. A swamp will do.

3. Make sure it doesn't rot away completely. It should be covered by layers of more half-rotted horsetails.

4. Squash down really hard, and leave to simmer gently under the ground for a good length of time, say about 350 million years. Oh, and don't forget to keep adding more layers of mud and sand.

5. Remove from the ground and burn.

You should find that with all this squashing your horsetail has turned into hard black coal. But coal is simply carbon from the carbon dioxide taken in by the horsetail by photosynthesis all those years ago. Worth the wait, wasn't it?

Moving the Computer

The computer is designed for rugged durability. However, a few simple precautions taken when moving the computer will help assure trouble-free operation.

- Make sure all disk activity has ended before moving the computer.

- If a diskette is in the diskette drive, remove it.

- If a CD/DVD is in the CD-ROM/DVD-ROM drive, remove it. Also make sure the CD-ROM/DVD-ROM drawer is closed.

- Turn off the power to the computer.

- Disconnect all the peripherals before moving the computer.

- Close the display. (Do not pick up the computer by its display panel or back where the interface ports are located.)

- Close all port covers.

- Disconnect the AC adaptor if it is connected.

- Use the carrying case when transporting the computer. Check that the computer's battery pack is fully charged.

- To extend the amount of time you can work without having to find a power outlet, take an additional battery pack with you.

Horrible Science: Vicious Veg

by Nick Arnold

Toshiba *Satellite* Quickstart Manual: Moving the Computer

There are many occasions when we need to follow instructions. Instructional text is usually written in a straightforward and direct style, often in a series of short sentences. However, if you examine different types of instructions, you may find considerable variations in approach.

Read, Think and Write

1. In the extract from *Horrible Science* what are the instructions about?

2. What is the purpose of the extract from the computer manual?

3. Look at the Toshiba extract. Apart from the second and third points, what do you notice about the beginning of each sentence in the list?

4. Rewrite the second and third points in the Toshiba extract so that they follow the same pattern as the other instructions.

Hint
Think about the action in the instruction.

5. The instructions in the two extracts use only words, numbers and bullet points. What else might a set of instructions use to make the meaning clear?

6. What differences are there in the way the two extracts are written?

7. Write a list of all the actions you are asked to do throughout both sets of instructions.

8. Which of the two sets of instructions did you find easier to follow and understand? Justify your opinion with references from the text.

9. Make a list of all the technical words in the Toshiba extract.

10. Rewrite the computer instructions in a more 'chatty', friendly style to appeal to those people who are uncertain or worried about using technical equipment.

Read and Analyse

1. Using a thesaurus, develop a word bank of verbs by finding synonyms for the verbs in each extract.

Hint
Look at the beginnings of sentences. There should be at least eight verbs you can investigate.

2. Write the instructions to 'Moving the Computer' as though you have completed them. Note what happens to the verbs.

Start your writing like this:
- I made sure all disk activity was ended before I moved the computer.
- As there was a diskette in the diskette drive, I removed it.
- There was a CD in the CD-ROM drive so I removed it. I also made sure the CD-ROM drive was securely closed ...

3. Write six sentences. In each one, repeat one of the words you have used, but add a prefix to give it the opposite meaning.

> **Example**
> Coal is organic in its structure, but computers are *in*organic.

Read, Discuss and Act

1. How many different situations can you think of where written instructions are needed? It is not always appropriate to use written instructions. What sort of situations require verbal instructions? What other methods of giving instructions can you think of?

2. Work together in a small group to develop a scene where following instructions is the central part of the narrative or action. Possible settings might be: an airport or aeroplane, a school, a hospital or first-aid centre. Either present your ideas as a group storytelling activity or act out the scene.

Food of the Sun

Grilled vegetables

The most prosaic titles can conceal the most extraordinary culinary revelations. Grilled vegetables are sensational fare and so easy to do that they should not be left to restaurants to profit from. Where food-writers, too frequently, gild their lilies with purple prose to sell an idea, here is one that readily sells itself without hyperbole.

Grilled vegetables? It is a functional and accurate description, but one that conceals a rich and fertile ground of opportunity, a simple technique which delivers the goods every time. It is not *haute cuisine*, just great food. All you need is a ridged grill pan or a barbecue. For dressing, nothing more than lemon juice, a little garlic and some good olive oil. A large plate covered in grilled vegetables makes a splendid summer lunch.

Ingredients

2 garlic cloves
150ml/¼ pt extra-virgin
   olive oil, plus more
   for brushing and
   serving
2 red sweet peppers
2 yellow sweet peppers
4 small aubergines
4 courgettes
4 large field mushrooms
2 large onions
16 halves of Oven-dried
   Tomatoes
   (see page 61)
2 lemons
salt and pepper
12 large basil leaves,
   to garnish

Preparation

Peel, and chop the garlic and put into a bowl. Pour olive oil over the garlic and stir. Leave to infuse. Preheat a ridged grilling pan or barbecue.

Grill the peppers whole over a flame or on a very hot ridged grill pan, turning frequently, till charred and blistered. Put them in a bowl, cover with cling film or a lid and leave for 20 minutes until the steam they generate loosens the blackened and blistered skins. Pull out the stem, which will come away neatly with the seeds. Cut the flesh into bite-sized rectangles and use to cover the centre of a serving dish, alternating yellow with red.

Slice the aubergine lengthwise. Grill these slices dry until soft, brown and blistered. Arrange around the peppers. Top and tail the courgettes and, if small, cut in half lengthwise. If large, cut into 4 slices. Grill dry, starting on the cut surfaces and turning at intervals until done.

Peel and remove the stems from the mushrooms. Grill dry, cap side down, until the beads of moisture start to exude into the stem point. Turn and cook the underside for 1 minute. Then transfer to paper towels, cap upwards, to drain. Slice the onion across into solid discs, discarding the ends. Turn the heat right down, brush the onion discs with oil and grill them slowly, otherwise they will burn on the outside before they are cooked through. Arrange them overlapping down the centre of the plate.

Conclude by butterflying the home-dried tomatoes by cutting them almost all the way through their middles and grill briefly, turning once.

Season the vegetables with salt and pepper, dress with the juice of one of the lemons, then dribble the garlic-infused olive oil over all of them. Pour over more oil if you think this amount looks weedy.

Serving

Scatter basil over and serve at room temperature with a wedge of lemon for everybody.

Oven-Baked Wild Mushroom Risotto

Serves 6 as a starter

I've always loved real Italian risotto, a creamy mass with the rice grains 'al dente' – but oh, the bother of all that stirring to make it. Then one day I was making a good old-fashioned rice pudding and I thought, why not try a risotto in the oven?

Why not indeed – it works like a dream and leaves you in peace to enjoy the company of your friends while it's cooking. I have since discovered, in fact, that in Liguria they do make a special kind of baked risotto called 'arrosto', so my version turns out to be quite authentic after all.

½ oz (10 g) dried porcini mushrooms (see page 233)
8 oz (225 g) fresh dark-gilled mushrooms
2½ oz (60 g) butter
1 medium onion, finely chopped
6 oz (175 g) Italian canaroli rice (risotto rice)
5 fl oz (150 ml) dry Madeira
2 tablespoons freshly grated Parmesan (Parmigiano reggiano), plus 2 oz (50 g) extra, shaved
   into flakes with a potato peeler
Salt and freshly milled black pepper

You will also need a 9-inch (23-cm) shallow ovenproof dish of 2½-pint (1.5-litre) capacity, approximately 2 inches (5 cm) deep. Pre-heat the oven to gas mark 2, 300°F (150°C).

First of all you need to soak the dried mushrooms, and to do this you place them in a bowl and pour 1 pint (570 ml) of boiling water over them. Then just leave them to soak and soften for half an hour. Meanwhile chop the fresh mushrooms into about ½-inch (1-cm) chunks – not too small, as they shrink down quite a bit in the cooking.

Now melt the butter in a medium saucepan, add the onion and let it cook over a gentle heat for about 5 minutes, then add the fresh mushrooms, stir well and leave on one side while you deal with the porcini. When they have had their half-hour soak, place a sieve over a bowl, line the sieve with a double sheet of absorbent kitchen paper and strain the mushrooms, reserving the liquid. Squeeze any excess liquid out of them, then chop them finely and transfer to the pan to join the other mushrooms and the onion. Keep the heat low and let the onions and mushrooms sweat gently and release their juices which will take about 20 minutes. Meanwhile put the dish in the oven to warm.

Now add the rice and stir it around to get a good coating of butter, then add the Madeira, followed by the strained mushroom-soaking liquid. Add a level teaspoon of salt and some freshly milled black pepper, bring it up to simmering point, then transfer the whole lot from the pan to the warmed dish. Stir once then place it on the centre shelf of the oven without covering. Set a timer and give it 20 minutes exactly.

After that, gently stir in the grated Parmesan, turning the rice grains over. Now put the timer on again, and give it a further 15 minutes, then remove from the oven and put a clean tea-cloth over it while you invite everyone to be seated. Like soufflés, risottos won't wait, so serve *presto pronto* on warmed plates and sprinkle with shavings of Parmesan.

Sookhi Bhaji

Potatoes with mustard seeds

A Hindu dish, this is served with Goan bread '*pao*', or with fluffy *pooris* at most neighbourhood stalls. It is generally ladled out into small saucers which serve as plates. You just dip your bread into it and eat. A popular place to find this combination of '*bhaji-pao*' is in the heart of Mapusa market at Café Corner, where local vendors, itinerant tribespeople and tourists all seem to want to come and eat. The place is jammed – and with good reason. The price is good (very cheap) and the taste of the food quite excellent.

Sookhi bhaji is eaten for breakfast, for lunch and even at tea-time! In fact, a cup of steaming milky tea tastes particularly good with it.

> **3 tablespoons vegetable oil**
> **1 teaspoon cumin seeds**
> **1 teaspoon brown mustard seeds**
> **1 medium-sized onion (75 g/3 oz), peeled and finely chopped**
> **2–4 fresh hot green chillies, split into halves lengthways**
> **4 small–medium waxy potatoes (450 g/1 lb), boiled, peeled and cut into 1 cm/½ inch dice**
> **1 teaspoon ground cumin**
> **1 teaspoon ground coriander**
> **½ teaspoon ground turmeric**
> **1 teaspoon salt**
> **¼ teaspoon cayenne pepper**
> **1 tablespoon finely chopped, fresh green coriander**

Heat the oil in a wide pan over medium-high heat. When hot, put in the cumin seeds and mustard seeds. As soon as the mustard seeds begin to pop, a matter of a few seconds, put in the onion and chillies. Turn the heat to medium. Stir and cook until the onion is quite soft but not brown. Put in the potatoes, ground cumin, coriander, turmeric, salt and cayenne pepper. Stir gently once or twice. Add 150 ml/5 fl oz/⅔ cup water and cook over medium-low heat for 8–10 minutes, stirring now and then, until all the spices have been absorbed by the potatoes. There should be just a hint of sauce at the bottom of the pan. Sprinkle the fresh coriander over the top, stir it in and serve.

Serves 4

Nothing much has changed in the veg world over the last year and a half, since my first book, but I still believe a lot of good things are going to happen in general supermarkets and markets. I've heard a few rumours that certain supermarkets think they're going to be 90 per cent organic by 2005, which is great. I wouldn't worry about price either, because as we buy more British produce, grown properly as it used to be before we started cheating and churning it out, it will become nice and cheap so everyone can afford it. Also, the variety of vegetables like cabbages, potatoes and tomatoes, as well as salad leaves, is slowly getting better. Things that could only be bought for restaurant use before are now popping up in supermarkets and that's superb.

I have noticed people's curiosity about cooking becoming more intense, which is great. I think a lot of people are now beginning to learn a lot about cooking and are really enjoying it, though sometimes when I walk round the supermarket I see such a massive contrast in buyers and I'm sure that will always be the case. In general I'll see young couples with their trolleys full of quite interesting vegetables – asparagus, artichokes, rocket – talking and sometimes arguing about the best combinations and ways to cook their veg for dinner. I find it so interesting. Usually they have some really good ideas, but others are definite no-nos and I do feel the urge to go up to them and say, 'Excuse me, I'm Dr Naked Chef, can I possibly help?' But I know they would just turn round and say, 'Who are you? On yer bike, mate!' The main thing, though, is that they are interested and they are trying. However, I can never get over the mother with lots of pasty kids and a trolley full of Coke, crisps and tinned spaghetti hoops. I feel like kidnapping the kids and force-feeding them vegetables for a month to get some colour back into their cheeks. ... At the end of the day, their diet is only as good as that of their parents.

Baked fennel with garlic butter and vermouth

This dish is so quick. I made it the other day, chucked it together and it's really light and flavoursome. It goes fantastically well with any meat or fish.

Serves 4

3 large heads of fennel
1 glove of garlic, finely sliced
3 large knobs of butter
2 wine glasses of vermouth
  (white wine also works)
salt and freshly ground black pepper

Preheat the oven to 220°C/425°F/gas 7. Remove any discoloured parts of the fennel, then cut the tops off and slice finely, reserving the leaves. I normally slice each fennel from the top to the root, into about 4 pieces, but it's not that important. You can slice them finer and more delicately if you like. Literally throw all the ingredients except the reserved leaves into a baking dish. Rip off a piece of greaseproof paper, run it under cold water and scrunch it up to make it soft. Then place it snugly over and around the fennel, not the actual dish. This bakes and steams the fennel at the same time – basically making it damn tasty! Cook in the preheated oven for 20 minutes, or until tender. Scatter with the fennel leaves before serving.

Food of the Sun

by Alastair Little and Richard Whittington

Delia Smith's Winter Collection

Madhur Jaffrey's Flavours of India

The Return of the Naked Chef

by Jamie Oliver

Cookery books are one of the most prolific forms of instructional writing. The presentation of the instructions is often influenced by the writer's style. In fact, cookery books have become an entertaining and interesting 'genre' to read, even by people who have a fear and loathing of cooking utensils and prefer to invest in a take-away pizza!

1. In the 'Grilled Vegetables' recipe from *Food of the Sun*, what should be done to the red and yellow peppers?

2. Why does Delia Smith think risottos are like soufflés?

3. What should be absorbed into the potatoes and what should be left at the bottom of the pan in Madhur Jaffrey's recipe for 'Potatoes with Mustard Seeds'?

4. Which part of the fennel should be removed and which part should be reserved in Jamie Oliver's 'Baked Fennel' recipe?

5. Give examples of the colloquial style that Jamie Oliver uses in his recipe instructions.

6. What do Alastair Little and Richard Whittington mean in the opening sentence of the introduction to their recipe?

7. What sort of mushrooms does Delia Smith use in her recipe and which ones do you cook first?

8. How and when is the dish 'Potatoes with Mustard Seeds' served?

9. Which set of instructions do you think is the easiest to follow? Use references from the extract to support your opinion.

10. Jamie Oliver has used an extended piece of writing to introduce each section of his book. Summarise the views he expresses in this introduction to vegetables.

11. What do you notice about the ingredients of all the recipes? Which of these dishes would you enjoy eating the most?

Read and Analyse

1. (a) Make a list of all the instructional verbs in the extracts. How many different ones can you find?

> **Examples**
> melt, add, peel.

(b) Use a thesaurus to find a suitable synonym for each verb.

> **Examples**
> add – combine, peel – skin

2. Each writer has a different style. Identfy the writer of each of these sentences and write down the meaning of the underlined words.

(a) A popular place to find this <u>combination</u> of '*bhaji-pao*' is in the heart of Mapusa market at Café Corner, where local <u>vendors</u>, <u>itinerant</u> tribespeople and tourists all seem to want to come and eat.

(b) Where food-writers, too frequently, <u>gild</u> their lilies with purple <u>prose</u> to sell an idea, here is one that readily sells itself without <u>hyperbole</u>.

(c) <u>Literally</u> throw all the ingredients except the <u>reserved</u> leaves into a baking dish.

3. Either choose one of the recipes to write in your own style or write your own recipe. Write an introduction which will persuade and encourage the reader to try the recipe. Consider style of layout for both the ingredients and the instructions for preparation.

Hint
Think about use of paragraphs, numbering, bullet points and headings.

Read, Discuss and Act

1. In a small group, talk about the following points:

- Do you agree with the points Jamie Oliver is making about buying vegetables? What are your own views?

- Madhur Jaffery's book is about food from India. Many different foods are available in Britain now. Discuss which foods you associate with which country.

- 'In Britain food is a form of entertainment; in some countries it is a matter of survival.' What truth is there in that statement?

2. In a small group, role-play the following scene. You are talking round a table in a restaurant. You are impressed with the meal and ask to meet the chef. The chef comes to your table and you question him/her on how he/she made the dish you admire. You could use one of the extracts to help structure the dialogue in your scene.

1 Modern wood stains are easy to app[ly], come in a wide choice of colours, and c[an] transform even existing timber features [into] something stylish. Finishes vary from natural wood shades to pretty pastels a[nd] strong, dramatic colours.

modern decked ## *pond*

With its bright blue flowers and glossy foliage, pickerel weed makes a bold statement between deck and pond.

This striking modern garden—given over completely to pond and decking—has a rich red and black theme softened by deep green foliage. Designer Henk Weijers has made excellent use of what is only a small space by defying the more conventional use of white paint and pale shades to create the impression of space and enclosing the area with a high, horizontally lapped fence stained Chinese red.

Far from being imposing, the atmosphere is warm and secluded, the perfect foil for a large, cool, deck-rimmed pool. The basic framework may be formal, but the boundaries of water, plants, seating, sculpture and walkways are indistinguishable from one another, the areas melting one into the other. There is nothing random about the planting either: although the overall effect is one of leafy abundance, plants are chosen and planted with precision. Softening the fence is a spectacular variegated *Miscanthus* alongside feathery, spreading bamboo; stands of upright *Pontederia* (pickerel weed) grow in dense rows alongside the dramatic decking). Even the seating and a sculptural feature marking the edge of the pond are part of the overall plan and treated to a matching stain.

▲ **2** Pondside sculpture: whether a classical figure or the modern pyramid t[hat] doubles as a decking rail in this garden, an artistic structure beside a pond make[s] an excellent focal point and unusual water reflections.

◀ **3** Pickerel wee[d] (*Pontederia cordata*) a pond plant th[at] is popular wi[th] designers too[.] Planted *en ma[sse]* it makes a su[perb] fringe of brig[ht] blue spikes.

▶ **4** Flowering rush (*Butomus umbellatus*) is an elegant way to add height to your pond margins with the bonus of showy pink parasol-like flowers in spring.

HE CAST OF CHARACTERS

3 Purple
strife (*Lythrum*
tum) makes a
tacular show of
and purple flower
s along the
rside. It is a
rous grower,
onsidered a
in the wild.

Astilbes are pretty perennials that
moist soil beside ponds and streams.
produce feathery foliage and plumes
y white, pink or red flowers.

◀ **7** Iris are wonderfully
dramatic pondside
characters with their large
sword-shaped foliage and
beautiful butterfly
blooms.

▼ **8** Spiderwort (*Tradescantia x
andersoniana*) makes good ground cover
with its low-growing, fleshy foliage dotted
with white, pink or purple flowers.

9 Poolside
walkway: a decked
walkway or paved
pathway around
the pond provides
year-round access
and many points of
interest.

▲ **10** With its
gold and green
striped fronds,
Eulalia (*Miscanthus
sinensis* 'Zebrinus')
is a wonderful
ornamental grass for
background interest.

▶ **12** There are 80
species of bamboo
(*Phyllostachys*),
many of which make
an excellent focal
point in the water
garden with their
tall, architectural,
woody stems and
fluttering foliage.

▶ **11** Log edging:
log piles create
a semi-formal look
and complement
decking and other
wooden features
in the garden.

ETTING THE SCENE

PLANTING

lants are essential in this garden to
often the structural features. Popular
designer' plants, with their dramatic
oliage and occasionally brilliant flowers,
ave been used singly to create a focal
oint or planted in rows or blocks for
xtra effect. If you want to emulate this
esign, try limiting your choice to just
few varieties and planting them *en
asse* or keeping to a two- or three-
olour scheme for plants and features.

OUNDARIES

oo often, boundary walls and fences
re considered little more than a
ecessity and miss out on any kind
f decorative treatment. With so many
arden paints and stains available, the
ptions are infinite: from natural timber
ffects to a weather-beaten bleached
nish or strong jewel-like reds, greens
nd blues. If the effect is too dominant,
often it with a little vertical planting.

DECKING

The beauty of decking is its flexibility:
it can be extended around virtually any
shape of formal pond and extended
to create fully integrated walkways,
seating areas, planting areas and even
sculptural features. Choosing a black
stain is a bold move, but here it has
a levelling effect on the deep red and
creates a dark, mysterious setting for
plants and fish. Another shade, or even
a plain timber stain, would have created
quite a different look.

POND DESIGN

If space is limited, it pays to think big
when it comes to ponds. Giving most of
the garden over to light-reflecting water
with walkways, bridges and stepping
stones to link different areas can create
the impression of space far more
effectively than the fragmented effect
of lots of little features and a tiny pond.

Water Garden Design

BEHIND THE SCENES

CONSTRUCTING A FORMAL SQUARE POND

A formal pond makes a fabulous focal point in the garden or on the patio, and can be any size and geometric shape, depending on your building skills. Link the shape to surrounding planting beds or build a series of ponds in complementary shapes.

① Calculate the size of your proposed pond, adding an extra 10 cm (4 in) in depth and 20 cm (8 in) in width. Excavate the hole, checking your angles and measurements at every stage.

② Create a concrete wall foundation in the hole around the bottom. Soak the base and add a 5 cm (2 in) layer of rubble. Pour in the wet concrete as smoothly as possible 10 cm (4 in) deep. Use a tamping block to level it at the top before it begins to spill. Leave it to dry and harden for at least 24 hours.

③ Using the base as a foundation, build and mortar a wall of two layers of concrete blocks about 45 cm x

22 cm x 10 cm (18 in x 9 in x 4 in). Fill any gaps between the blocks and the soil with concrete mix.

④ Drape flexible liner over the hole and secure it around the edge with bricks. Pull the creases together and fold them into the corners. Make up a concrete mix of 4 parts clean 1 cm (0.5 in) chippings, 2 parts sand and 1 part cement. Spread and level 5 cm (2 in) of the mix over the base and foundations. Leave for 24 hours.

⑤ Drape 2.5 cm (1 in) chicken wire over the edge of the pool down to the base, ensuring there are no sharp edges. Mortar two layers of house bricks onto the lined concrete block wall on top of the chicken wire, using a spirit level. Support the liner with backfill up behind the house bricks to make sure the water level remains well above the visible liner. Leave to dry for 2 days.

⑥ Strengthen the structure by plastering a 1-cm (0.5-in) layer of fibre-reinforced cement on the inside of the pool. The chicken wire will hold it in place.

⑦ After two days, paint the inside of the pool with a waterproof sealant designed to neutralise the lime content of the cement.

POINTS TO REMEMBER

● Do not attempt this style of construction unless you have had experience working with these materials before.

● Never work in wet weather or if there is any risk of frost. Cover your work with a sheet or piece of tarpaulin overnight in any case.

● When making a formal shape, double-check your measurements and angles at every stage to be sure there are no errors, because they will be difficult to disguise later.

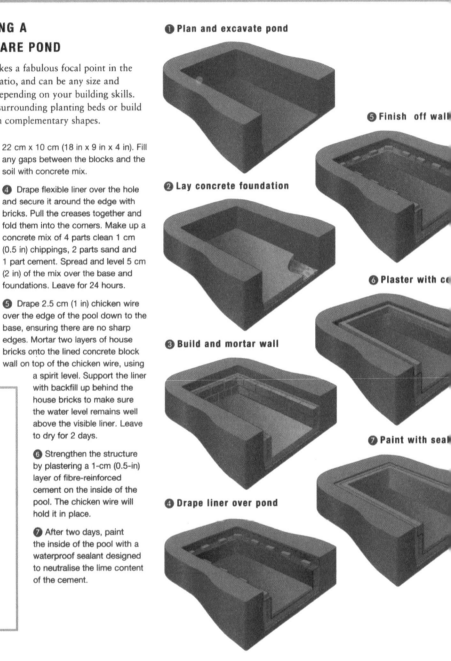

① Plan and excavate pond

② Lay concrete foundation

③ Build and mortar wall

④ Drape liner over pond

⑤ Finish off wall

⑥ Plaster with ce[ment]

⑦ Paint with seal[ant]

TIMBER EDGING AND DECKED BRIDGE

Timber in the garden has a lovely soft effect in contrast to harder landscaping materials such as stone and paving. Use it as an edging material, or to build decked walkways and bridges to be stained the colour of your choice.

1 At 0.5 m (18-in) intervals, drill into the top of the brickwork. Insert rawl plugs and screw the timber edging into place with brass or galvanised screws.

2 Dig two holes each side of the pond for the 30 cm (12 in) square joists. They will need to be 1.2 m (4 ft) apart. Fill with 10 cm (4 in) of rubble topped with a 10-cm (4-in) layer of concrete.

3 Once the concrete has hardened, steel joist shoes or brackets can be bolted into place using 5 cm (2 in) wall bolts. Level the timber uprights or bearers. Nail the bearers into place, flat side down.

4 Fix the joists at right angles to the bearers, 45 cm (18 in) apart with nails at an angle of 45 degrees. You can then nail your bridge timbers into position on top.

Flowering rush

▲ Timber can be used to enhance the garden in many ways. Here it makes a striking water feature overhead as well as underfoot.

1 Screw down timber edging

3 Attach timber uprights and bearers

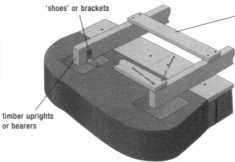

'shoes' or brackets   joists

timber uprights or bearers

2 Create joist foundations

4 Nail bridge timbers into position

POINTS TO REMEMBER

● When bolting concrete shoes onto cured concrete, predrilling the holes will ease fixing.

● Ask your supplier whether treated timber is safe for use beside or over water. Some treatments can be toxic to fish and plants.

● Decking timber with a reeded surface is preferable for bridges because it is less likely to be slippery in wet weather.

Water Garden Design

Welcome to
computer arts
Britain's biggest-selling creative magazine ▸ Mac & PC

Fantastic
effects in
Photoshop

OUR AWESOME COVER IMAGE
HIGHLIGHTS THE DEPTH OF
PHOTOSHOP, PARADING MANY
LAYERS, 3D AND COMPOSITING
EFFECTS. WANT TO KNOW HOW
IT'S DONE? THEN READ ON...

This issue's cover tutorial has gone all mysterious and eerie – the complete opposite to the known powers of Adobe's leading software package.

This tutorial starts with the background and works up, giving you a feel for the image and giving the illustration that added bit of depth too. And, as well as utilising the thunder of *Photoshop*, it also gives you the chance to practise some hocus pocus with multiple programs and plug-ins, plus shareware and freeware packages. (Don't discard those old 3D packages, they may still have a use.)

This tutorial shows you how to mix up a model, some letters, a plastic sheet and a few bits of software to create the unearthly cover image.

All the files you need are included in Dual\Tutorial\Cover Tutorial. There's a demo of *Photoshop* on the CD, plus a demo of the *Alien Skin* plug-in and *form•Z 3*. There are other packages used too, but no demo – if you've got the package, have a go yourself – otherwise the CD files for these parts are all on the CD. Let the jiggery pokery commence...

Artwork & expertise supplied by Jacey. You can contact him via Debut Art on ☎ 0171 636 1064, ✉ jc@jacey.com or point your browser towards W www.jacey.com

Stage one: **Getting started**

We created the background for this stage using a photograph of a plastic bag. If the file size and dimensions are too big for your computer, just halve everything. For the completed stage see the file bckground1.psd...

1 We start off with a high-res photo of some plastic sheet wrapping. It gives good tonal ranges when used for a background – but if you want to use something else, try scanning objects or any textured photos. Alternatively, open scan.tif in *Photoshop*.

2 We now adjust the image to get rid of the dull grey colours. Open the Hue/Saturation dialog box – set the Hue to 209, and Saturation to 56. (You can use a different colour if you want to). Once you've done that, use the Radial Blur filter set at 16, Blur method clicked to Zoom, and Quality set at Good. Now we have the basis of our background.

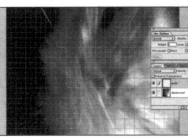

3 Look at any cool designs or illustrations th[...] days, and you'll see they have grids or horizo[...] lines. There are a number of ways to create grids i[...] *Photoshop*, and here's one of them. First, create a layer. Open Preferences>Guides and Grids, then se[...] Gridline every 0.6cm and sub-divisions every 0.6cm[...] Now view Grid and select the Line tool (set at one [...] thick), and anti-alias switches off.

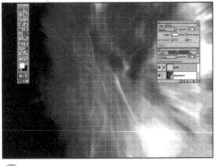

4 Select the colour White as your foreground line colour. Now, using the Line tool (and holding Shift to constrain the lines), match the grid with the Line tool. Trace the vertical and horizontal lines. Once done, set the Layer mode to Overlay.

5 Switch off grids. Duplicate the layer, then apply Gaussian Blur to the new layer at around 2.8. Select the Pointer tool, and using your mouse or arrow keys, offset the blurred grid by about 4-8 pixels.

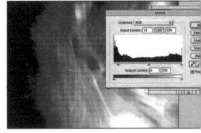

6 Now flatten the image and adjust the level[...] the above dialog box. Here, we're just giving [...] background a bit more depth. Once that's done, sa[...] image as bckground1.psd (it's on the CD). Then clo[...] the window and *Photoshop* (if you don't have enou[...] memory to open two applications). You wouldn't normally flatten the image, but as it's a tutorial an[...] you don't want to make any changes, go ahead.

Stage two: **3D frames**

Here's how to make complex-looking frames in a 3D package or a plug-in (*Alien Skin* is on the CD). See CD files in Stage 2.

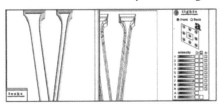

1 Using your 3D app's Type tool, create the letters V, C and O in separate documents and give them a metallic-looking texture render with a mask/alpha channel and no shadows (or see the CD files in Stage 2). Use any typeface you want (we used Courier) for the O, and Bookman for V and C. Render V and C at around 3.3x3.3cm, 300dpi; and O at around 5x5cm. Don't worry about colours for now.

2 Now prepare them for 'chopping up' and 'repeating'. Open your rendered letters, then create a selection or load the selection from the appropriate channel using the Magic Wand. Then cut, copy and paste them in to new documents. Use Colourise in Hue/Saturation (Image menu) to get the desired blue effect (or use a colour you prefer). Delete unwanted background layers and save each letter as v.psd, o.psd and c.psd.

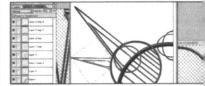

3 Now create a new document at 4x4cm, 300[...] Here, you'll cut sections from your letters an[...] use them to create a similarly layered shape as the[...] above image. Don't worry about naming layers, but [...] may need to duplicate some of them. Use Transfor[...] rotate and scale the elements. Once you've create[...] shape, you can delete the background layer and m[...] existing layers. Save the file as cornerfr1.psd (che[...] out on the CD). Close files c.psd and v.psd.

84

...age two: 3D frames continued...

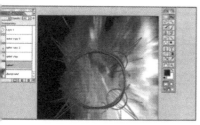

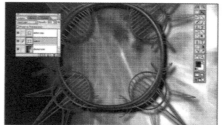

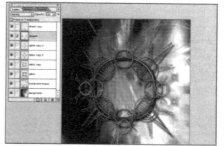

Open bckground1.psd (Stage 1 folder) and ...select, copy and paste the o.psd image into the ...ground (do the same for the cornerfr1.psd). ...rnatively, just drag-and-drop their layers in to ...ile and call it spike1. Now duplicate the spike1 ..., do this three more times & flip vertically and ...ontally to get the same shape as above. Then ...ge all the layers (excluding the background).

5   Duplicate the layer again. Select the layer above the background and select Preserve Transparency in the Layers palette. Go to Edit>Fill and fill 100% black. Switch off Preserve Transparency and set the layer to Hard light. Set Gaussian Blur at around 7. Use the Pointer tool to offset your newly made drop shadow. Position to suit the depth of shadow, as above.

6   Repeat the last two stages with more shapes, even duplicating and reducing the main frame or adding your own shapes. Use some shapes set as Hard light and screen below the main shapes. Now flatten the image and save. See shapebck.tif on the CD.

...age three: Weird shapes

...w we're going to use a variety of plug-ins and filters to create blobs and spheres to go in the frame (if you don't have the ...ware, CD files are supplied). See the Stage 3 folder on the CD – the Weird Shape folder for files and orbbck1.psd...

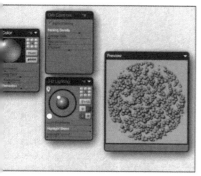

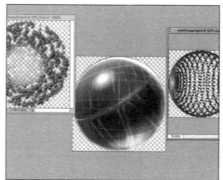

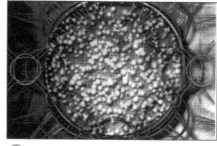

►   Create a new document about 2x2cm. Then, ...using *Kai's Power Tools'* Orbit and Spheroid ...gner, create a number of weird shapes. (If you ...have this, use the CD files provided.)

2   Use anything you like that helps create the above shapes. Don't worry if you don't have any of these – see Weird Shapes 1-4.psd on the CD.

3   Here, we've used a *KPT 5* Orbit image and placed it in the centre of the image (see weirdshape1.psd). Scale the image up to fit more in the middle of the frame, and use Gaussian Blur to soften it. Set the Layer mode to Hard light. Duplicate the layer, set Opacity to 44 and Layer mode to Colour Dodge. Now move it below the layer you used to duplicate it.

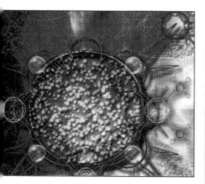

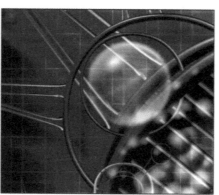

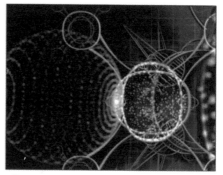

Now use the other weird shapes, and place ...them around the frame. It doesn't have to be as ...etrical as we've made it – just experiment and ...them where you want.

5   Set weirdshape2.psd to screen. A simple spheroid now looks like a glowing crystal.

6   Set this one to screen as well. Using more shapes and the Orbit again, you can get some odd effects by merging the shapes together and playing around with Layer modes.

Water Garden Design

by Yvonne Rees and Peter May

'Fantastic effects in Photoshop'

Computer Arts magazine

Instructional texts are presented in many different styles and formats. They often assume a certain level of interest and expertise on the part of the reader, by the language they use. The two texts in this section both give instructions for design, but on two very different subjects. One provides instructions on how to create a water feature for a garden, while the other gives instructions which describe how to produce a particular image using computer software.

Read, Think and Write

1. Who designed the modern decked pond featured in the extract from *Water Garden Design* and how has he made excellent use of a small space?

2. If space is limited, why does it pay to think big when it comes to pond design?

3. Write down three ways in which timber can be used in the design. Why should care be taken when using this material?

Hint
Check the second 'Points to Remember'.

4. Write a paragraph naming the plants that the designer has chosen for his design and explaining why he has chosen them.

5. Rewrite the paragraph that starts 'Far from being imposing ...' in your own words.

6. What has been used to create the background of the computer-generated design?

7. What tools are used at stage one of the design?

8. What happens to the letters created at stage two of the design?

9. What software is used to create a number of weird shapes at stage three of the design?

10. What happens to 'a simple spheroid'? How can you get some other odd effects with shapes?

Read and Analyse

1. Make two lists. One should be a list of all the instructional verbs from the text and diagram captions of the 'Behind the Scenes' section of the garden design extract. The other should be a list of all the instructional verbs from the stage-by-stage tutorial in the computer design extract. Are there any similarities between them? What differences are there?

Hint
The verb 'create' will appear in both lists.

2. Write a comparison of the format and layout of the two texts. In your conclusion give your opinion on which text you found more interesting and which was easier to follow. The computer text is an extract so remember that you have not got all the instructions to create the final image.

3. Using the format and layout of one of the texts as a model, write your own instructions for a real or 'virtual' garden feature.

Read, Discuss and Act

1. What other areas might make use of computer-generated designs? What advantages are there in using this method of design? Are there any disadvantages? In a small group, discuss the possibilities that are offered by the use of computers in the processes of designing and making.

2. Gardening programmes have become increasingly popular. Does the personality of the presenter help to gain viewers' interest? Use the water garden text as a 'script' and, in a small group, act out a 'task-force'-style programme in which you have to build a modern decked garden under the pressure of a time limit. What sort of personalities will your presenters have? Will they work together well to produce the desired result or will the time limit create problems?

AMAZING OFFER

Calling all intelligent Game Players...

CLONE ALONE

The board game which allows you to make more of yourself. Show your true potential by building a team of 'selves' to defeat the team your opponent constructs.

For this amazingly low price of £25.00, you will receive the following:

- Lots of easy to loose plastic bits
- A board which will never fold back into its box
- Easy to follow instructions (if you have a degree in biochemistry and genetics)
- All packaged in a state of the art cardboard box.

SPECIAL OFFER

BUY TWO GAMES AND GET A FREE BOOK WHICH EVEN BOYS WILL WANT TO READ

GAME OF THE CENTURY

Yes, we know it's only 2001 but the century has already produced the ultimate in a game. Scientist and father of four, John Urstwhile, predicts this game will never be bettered in the future. *'I predict this game will never be bettered. It has all the ingredients of a classic,'* he said at the Chippenham and County Games Fair.

We are able to offer this inspiring game at a low price owing to our clever over-ordering policy. Do not delay – fill in the form below and send money.

BUY NOW WHILE STOCKS ARE TOO LARGE

Clip and mail
Send money to: **CLONE ALONE Offer, The Industrial Estate, Madrigal Road, London.**

Name ....

Address ....

DON'T FORGET THE MONEY

"I'll have a Perrier and water, please."

Quite how the barman at New York's Algonquin Hotel reacted to this young lady's order we shall never know.

We reacted with some horror, however.

Perrier with Scotch, certainly. Perrier with dinner, of course. Perrier on its own, naturally. But Perrier with water?

However, when we thought a little deeper about her predicament – a smart hotel, a special evening, perhaps a desire to impress her companion by ordering a drink with style – we decided that never again should Perrier be a cause of such embarrassment.

So, for aficionados and the uninitiated alike:

"Everything you always wanted to know about Perrier but never dared to ask."

At Vergèze, between the somnolent volcanoes of the Auvergne and the Mediterranean, lies a mineral water spring which was bubbling long before Hannibal and his thirsty elephants crossed the Alps and rested there.

Source Perrier.

The Romans built baths there, the French added a spa and hôtel, and, in 1863 Napoleon III decreed that the naturally sparkling spring water be bottled "for the good of France." (Clearly it didn't do him much harm.)

It's rather ironic, however, that it took an Englishman – and a car crash – to put Perrier where it is today.

St. John Harmsworth had bought the spa, spring and all, in 1903.

So, when he crashed his car in England three years later, where better to recuperate than his own sleepy spa in the South of France?

But, like Archimedes in the bath two thousand years before, the presence of so much water was to inspire him.

It occurred to him that, if people would come to Vergèze to take the waters, think how many would enjoy it if he took it to them? – Eureka!

Harmsworth promptly forgot the spa, and concentrated on giving Perrier the distinctive French livery by which it is recognised all over the world today.

The name. The classical logo. The unique Perrier bottle (based on the Indian clubs which he used for remedial exercise).

The water itself he left alone. For Man can add nothing to the natural sparkle which Nature has already provided.

Except a bottle to make sure it will travel well, and arrive as fresh as it left the source.

Which has made Perrier the ideal choice of bon viveurs, the perfect complement to good spirits, and the international hallmark of taste and good company.

No wonder our unfortunate lady was so eager to order it.

We hope the faux pas didn't ruin her evening.

And whether you're eating, drinking, trying not to drink, playing sport or staying at the Algonquin Hotel, we hope Perrier will add to yours.

A votre santé!

264

89

Clone Alone advertisement
Perrier advertisement

Advertising is the business of persuasion. Its use of visual layout, and its careful attempts to target an audience by an appropriate style of language to persuade them to buy a product, are the focus of our study of these two extracts. Check out the meaning of 'parody' before you start the activities.

Read, Think and Write

1. What is the product in the 'Clone alone' advertisement and what is the company that made it called?

2. What 'expert opinion' is used to promote the product?

3. Which words are repeated in the 'clip and mail' section?

4. '... get a free book which even boys will want to read.' What does that statement imply?

5. Give four examples from the Clone Alone text which show that it is making fun of advertising.

6. Where and how is the young lady's order recorded in the Perrier advertisement?

7. What pronoun defines the Perrier voice in the advert? What is the reaction to the young lady's order?

8. How has the Perrier advert used history to give the product the respectability of authority and tradition?

9. Make a list of expressions and words in the Perrier text which imply that only people with 'good taste' or who enjoy the 'good life' drink Perrier.

Hint
Check out your French!

10. Write a brief commentary on the Perrier advert, referring to its layout and the content of the text. How effective do you think it is? Would it persuade you to buy Perrier?

11. Design and write your own parody of an advert.

Read and Analyse

1. Which words, phrases or sections of the extracts would you put under these headings? Study each extract and write your examples under the appropriate heading.

   <u>Attention-grabbers</u>
   Slogans
   Headlines
   Captions
   Pictures

   <u>Techniques of persuasion</u>
   Claiming value
   Promoting self-image
   Special offers
   Use of an expert's opinion or authority

2. Imagine you are going to produce an advertisement for a food product. Write a letter to a real or imaginary expert or famous person, explaining the merits of your product and requesting their support in endorsing the product. This is a business letter so use a formal tone and persuasive language to describe your product.

Hint
Use a thesaurus to find suitably impressive words to make your business proposition attractive.

Read, Discuss and Act

1. Do you find any types of advertising convincing? Do some adverts parody themselves? In a small group, compile a list of memorable adverts and discuss what makes them so. Is humour a quality that makes them memorable? How many of the adverts use famous people to 'back' the product? Are most of your examples television adverts or those you have seen in magazines? What other forms of advertising can you think of?

2. Working in a small group, use a tape recorder to create an advertisement to be broadcast on a local radio station. The subject should be either a food or a sports product. Advertising on air is expensive so your advert needs to be short but persuasive. In the planning consider what the product's main selling point is. If it's a food product, it might be its taste or its wholesome ingredients. If it's a sports product, it might be its 'self-image' qualities. Will you use humour? Will you bring in the backing of an expert or famous person?

The Observer 1 April 2001

Wanted: An outstanding Chief Executive…

to £130,000

Coventry was flattened in the war and was re-built. It was crushed by the demise of the manufacturing industries and was renewed. It is a symbol the world over of peace and reconciliation, of struggles and achievement against the odds.

The people of Coventry are exceptional. And they deserve nothing less from their council.

Coventry is already a well-run authority, with emerging areas of excellence, and takes a national lead in partnership working and neighbourhood renewal. But it is not consistently good and wants to be better throughout - a beacon authority, at the heart of a great city and the leading edge of best practice and modern local government.

Coventry has enormous potential, but also faces some big social challenges - an increasingly elderly population, too many children in care, and the need to ensure that everyone benefits from its economic renaissance and new-found prosperity.

As Chief Executive your job will be to develop and deliver a renewed vision

for the city and the council. You will be a champion for local democracy and the city. You will use performance management to drive up standards and spread best practice, and to tackle areas of weakness.

You will be the council's ambassador at regional, national and international levels. And you'll have to be a good manager too - capable of inspiring people to deliver a coherent vision. Not to mention being responsible for a net revenue budget of £309 million this year and a capital programme of £150 million over the next five years.

Coventry is constantly changing and you will need to drive that process, influence its direction and keep it on course.

You'll also need to share Coventry's strong values of quality services, social justice, good governance and government through partnership.

If you believe that you have the ambition, energy, vision, skills and enthusiasm to take Coventry's dreams and turn them into reality - we want to hear from you. Take the first step and download a briefing pack from our

advisors' website or call their 24 hour line on 020 7804 2774, quoting reference 4107G to obtain a hard copy. If you wish to have an informal or confidential discussion about the role, please call either Martin Tucker on 0121 265 6735 or Hamish Davidson on 020 7804 3115.
Closing date is Friday 6th April 2001.

PricewaterhouseCoopers
Executive Search & Selection
Cornwall Court
19 Cornwall Street
Birmingham B3 2DT
Fax: 0121 265 5575
Email:
hamish.davidson@uk.pwcglobal.com

Website:
www.pwcglobal.com/executive/uk

Coventry City Council

…to shape the dreams of an exceptional city

PRICEWATERHOUSE COOPERS
EXECUTIVE SEARCH & SELECTION

WILDLIFE SURVEY 2001

WWF-UK

Panda House
Weyside Park
Catteshall Lane
Godalming
Surrey GU7 1XR

Tel: 01483 426444
Fax: 01483 426409
www.wwf-uk.org

How much do you care about wildlife?

Dear Householder,

We know that Britain is an animal-loving nation. And we know that many people are aware of the threat to many species of animals in the wild. What we don't quite know is how strongly people feel about the threat - whether, for instance, they care more about tigers than they do about dolphins or whether they think that extinction of species is really important in a world which has so many human tragedies to deal with.

Your area has been selected as one in which we are trying to establish the reactions of ordinary British people to the issues of wildlife, the extinction of species and environmental matters in general. Many of your neighbours will be receiving this same questionnaire and I do hope you can find the time to complete it, for the answers you give us will be invaluable as we plan future campaigns to protect wildlife.

Continued overleaf/

Have you ever seen an otter in the wild?

There are less than 500 Siberian tigers left in the Russian Far East. Does it matter if they become extinct?

President: HRH Princess Alexandra, the Hon Lady Ogilvy GCVO
Chairman: the Hon Sara Morrison
Chief Executive: Robert Napier
WWF-UK Registered Charity Number 1081247
VAT Number GB 244 2516 81

Taking action for a living planet

WILDLIFE SURVEY 2001

WWF's position is quite clear. We are committed to help protect all species on Earth - mammals, fish, birds, plants and insects. That's why we are so alarmed at the rate at which many species are disappearing. And that is why we are mounting an ambitious campaign on behalf of the world's threatened species and habitats. But, hand in hand with that campaign to raise money for our work, we have decided to solicit your opinions on the subject.

Naturally, and because we are a charity, we are giving you the chance to become a supporter of WWF for as little as £2 a month. But do let me make it quite clear that we want your answers to this survey whether or not you decide to support WWF.

Hundreds of thousands will be involved in this research exercise. It will take you just a few minutes to answer these simple questions and the reply envelope enclosed will cost you nothing to send back.

Let me thank you in advance for your co-operation.

Yours sincerely

Robert Napier
Chief Executive, WWF-UK

How important is it to save him?

The end is in sight...unless we act now.

There is now no doubt that many of the world's species are in crisis. This year alone, we estimate that thousands will be wiped out, never to return.

The wolf is extinct in many European countries, threatened in others. The black rhino population has been decimated from 60,000 to 2,600 in just twenty years. The red squirrel is rarely seen in Britain today. And there are only around 5,000 tigers left in the wild.

WWF has been at the forefront of the fight to save endangered species for forty years now. We help protect the natural habitats of creatures throughout the world, from the seas of Antarctica to the rainforests in the Amazon. We work with governments and with local people to preserve nature in every aspect.

There have been many successes. You may already know that 30 million square miles of ocean around Antarctica has been declared a sanctuary for whales. And we are starting to see a decline in tiger poaching in Russia, where we have been supporting anti-poaching patrols.

But time is running out for the tiger and many other species. We need faster, more decisive action. And the best way for you to help is to join us.

How to join WWF.

£2 a month makes you a **Member** of WWF-UK. Every member will receive the beautiful tiger print pictured right, a Welcome Pack and a special member's certificate. Thereafter you will be sent a quarterly copy of 'WWF News' to keep you in touch with our work.

Picture by Ian Ledgerwood

Print size (210x297mm)

£5 a month makes you a **Companion** of WWF. In addition to all the gifts listed above you will receive a special panda lapel pin.

£10 a month makes you one of a select group of **Benefactors.** You will receive the tiger print, newsletter, panda lapel pin and a distinguished certificate to commemorate your very special contribution to our conservation work. You will also receive a free subscription to 'Living Planet' magazine and may be invited to special WWF events.

Your contribution counts. Call

08705 66 88 99

to set up a Direct Debit and join WWF today.

Registered Charity No. 1081247   100% recycled post-consumer waste paper

SUR0904

WILDLIFE SURVEY 2001

CONFIDENTIAL

Please try to answer all the questions, then fill in your name and address and send it back to WWF in the reply envelope enclosed. The form also gives you the opportunity to make a contribution to WWF's work.

1. If you keep any pets, what are they?

Dog ☐₁ Cat ☐₂ Bird ☐₃ Fish ☐₄ Other ☐₅

2. How important is wildlife to you?

Very important ☐₆ Important ☐₇ Not very important ☐₈

3. Do you think action should be taken to prevent the following from happening?

	Yes	No	Don't Know
Rhinos being poached in Zimbabwe for their horns	☐₉	☐₁₀	☐₁₁
Snow leopards poisoned in revenge by shepherds in Nepal	☐₁₂	☐₁₃	☐₁₄
Polar Bears dying in the Arctic because of melting ice	☐₁₅	☐₁₆	☐₁₇
Tigers being killed for traditional Chinese medicine	☐₁₈	☐₁₉	☐₂₀

4. How important is preserving the environment to you?

Very important ☐₂₁ Important ☐₂₂ Not very important ☐₂₃

5. Do you think the world should be concerned about any of these issues?

	Yes	No	Don't Know
The effects of climate change	☐₂₄	☐₂₅	☐₂₆
Leaving a better planet for our children	☐₂₇	☐₂₈	☐₂₉
The levels of toxins in food and drink	☐₃₀	☐₃₁	☐₃₂
Wild animals becoming extinct	☐₃₃	☐₃₄	☐₃₅
High levels of pollution	☐₃₆	☐₃₇	☐₃₈
Having clean water to drink	☐₃₉	☐₄₀	☐₄₁
Educating children about the environment	☐₄₂	☐₄₃	☐₄₄
Preserving natural resources such as forests	☐₄₅	☐₄₆	☐₄₇

6. Do you do any of the following?

	Yes	No	Don't Know
Use energy efficient appliances	☐₄₈	☐₄₉	☐₅₀
Use unleaded petrol	☐₅₁	☐₅₂	☐₅₃
Recycle packaging	☐₅₄	☐₅₅	☐₅₆
Buy organic or free range food items	☐₅₇	☐₅₈	☐₅₉
Buy wood products from sustainable forests	☐₆₀	☐₆₁	☐₆₂
Visit nature reserves or conservation areas	☐₆₃	☐₆₄	☐₆₅

7. Would you go whale watching in a country that supports the hunting of whales?

	Yes	No	Don't Know
	☐₆₆	☐₆₇	☐₆₈

8. Would you like to receive information on any of the following WWF products?

WWF/MBNA credit card (I23) ☐₆₉
WWF Guide to Making a Will (I04) ☐₇₀
Becoming a WWF volunteer (I18) ☐₇₁
Adopting a dolphin (23I)/rhino (I96)/
elephant (I93)/tiger (I91)/orang utan (I94) ☐₇₂
(please delete as appropriate)

9. What is your date of birth? _____

Mr/Mrs/Miss/Ms _____ Initials _____ Surname _____

Address _____

_____

_____ Postcode _____

Tel No: (inc STD) _____

Email address _____

D062

Gift Aid - please remember to ✔ when you give.

This government scheme adds tax relief to your donations. For every £1 you give today the government will add 28p from your taxes. It doesn't cost you a penny and when you tick this box today all of your gifts in future will also be topped up with Gift Aid.

☐ **Yes,** Please treat all my donations from 6th April 2000 and until further notice as Gift Aid.

I confirm I pay an amount of income tax and/or capital gains tax at least equal to the tax that WWF will reclaim on my donations in the tax year.

If you would like to support WWF in its work for threatened species and habitats, please complete this section, or call 08705 66 88 99. All calls are charged at national rates.

Here is my application to become a supporter of WWF.

Please tick the appropriate box

I would like to help protect our threatened species and habitats by becoming:

A WWF Member for £2 a month ☐

A WWF Companion for £5 a month ☐

A WWF Benefactor for £10 a month ☐

OR

I wish to make a monthly gift of £ ☐

OR

I would like to give £ [_____] to help protect our threatened species and habitats. I enclose a cheque/postal order made payable to WWF-UK ☐

Please tick box if you do not wish to receive your free tiger print ☐

We sometimes allow other organisations whose aims are in sympathy with our own to contact our supporters. If you do not wish to hear from them, please tick this box. ☐

Please tick this box if you do not wish to receive any further communications from WWF. ☐

(Under the terms of the Data Protection Act, you have the right to advise us at any time if you do not wish to receive further mailings from WWF, or organisations with whom we co-operate.) Registered Charity number 1081247.

PLEASE DO NOT DETACH

DIRECT DEBIT

Instruction to your Bank or Building Society to pay Direct Debits.

Originator's Identification | 9 | 9 | 1 | 4 | 7 | 3 |

5. WWF-UK Reference Number (Office use only)

1. Name and full postal address of your Bank or Building Society branch

To: The Manager _____ Bank or Building Society

Address _____ Postcode _____

2. Name(s) of account holder(s)

3. Branch sort code

☐☐ — ☐☐ — ☐☐

(from the top right hand corner of your cheque)

4. Bank or Building Society Account Number

☐☐☐☐☐☐☐☐

6. Instruction to your Bank or Building Society:
Please pay WWF-UK Direct Debits from the account detailed on this instruction subject to the safeguards assured by The Direct Debit Guarantee. I understand that this instruction may remain with WWF-UK and, if so, details will be passed electronically to my Bank/Building Society.

Signature _____

Date _____

Banks and Building Societies may not accept Direct Debit instructions for some types of accounts.

Please return this completed form to:
WWF-UK, FREEPOST, (GI 2122), Northampton, NN99 IWF.

Coventry City Council advertisement
WWF communication and survey

Texts that are written to attract the attention of a specific audience will also use persuasive language and appropriate layout techniques in order to achieve the required response. You may not feel you are quite ready to apply for the post advertised with Coventry City Council until you have gained more business skills. However, you may be persuaded to join the WWF after you have read their communication.

Read, Think and Write

1. How does the text of the advertisement make you feel that Coventry is a place with a remarkable and influential past?

2. How are the people of Coventry described?

3. How does the writer describe what Coventry has already achieved? What does it aim to achieve in the future?

4. What are the problems which Coventry faces?

5. Make a list of the things the Chief Executive will be expected to do.

6. Write down words or phrases from the advertisement which make the Chief Executive sound very special.

7. What steps is it suggested you take if you are interested in applying for the job?

8. Write a formal letter applying for the position of Chief Executive of Coventry City Council. Refer closely to the text to show your commitment to the needs of Coventry and its people.

9. Summarise the main points of the letter from WWF.

10. What successess are reported in the WWF information sheet?

11. What information is given about the species of animals that are in crisis?

12. How does the information sheet make joining WWF seem attractive?

Hint
Use a similar style and vocabulary to those of the text to achieve the appropriate tone.

Read and Analyse

1. Study the WWF letter and information sheet. Select ten persuasive words, phrases, sentences or format techniques and explain why you think they have been used.

2. Write the following phrases from the texts in your own words:
   (a) confidential discussion
   (b) a coherent vision
   (c) economic renaissance
   (d) solicit your opinions
   (e) a select group of benefactors
   (f) declared a sanctuary

3. You have succeeded in becoming the Chief Executive of a small business. You now need to persuade people to work for you. Design and write an advertisement describing what your business is and how potentially successful it will be. Decide which positions need to be filled, e.g. manager, secretary. What qualities do the applicants need to have?

Read, Discuss and Act

1. What do you think about the prospect of earning a living? Would you rather be the Chief Executive of a city council or of an organisation like WWF? Do you think some types of work have more value than others?

2. In a small group, discuss the questions in the WWF survey. Compile some questions of your own for a survey on people's opinions of work.

3. With a partner role-play the informal discussion offered in the Coventry City Council advertisement.

"You have been present during all these years with a constancy and dedication which has accompanied me in the worst moments giving me strength and joy. I remember clearly the emotion I felt on returning to my cell after one of the fortnightly visits, the only time I talked to anyone, having learned about your letters. The solidarity that is expressed over oceans of distance gives strength and faith in one's solitude...."

Lilian Celiberti,
from a letter to
Amnesty International, 1983.

the case that it is now closed. Sometimes, it may be that torture has stopped or a political prisoner's conditions have greatly improved. Sometimes a prisoner of conscience has been set free. Whatever the case involves, Amnesty is proud of the fact that until it gets what it is campaigning for, it never gives up.

When there's good news, the research department lets everyone involved know on notepaper headed "Closure of Case". These are sweet words to read. However, what happens to the prisoner's dossier depends on the case. If the person has been set free and is not in danger of being re-arrested, the dossier, which is confidential, must be destroyed. If there is still the threat of renewed torture or a worsening of conditions, the prisoner's group keeps the dossier in a safe place.

Sometimes, there is concern about the ex-prisoner's welfare. Some people, released into the world perhaps after many years of much brutal treatment, find it very hard to cope. Amnesty doesn't let these people down. It adopted them as prisoners, now it cares for them. For at least six months after a prisoner is freed, and sometimes even longer, Amnesty members help with money, food parcels and letters of support. Aftercare, as it is called, helps an ex-prisoner remember that although the case is closed, there are still people who care.

The death sentence

Although Amnesty cares about all the rights set down in the United Nations' declaration of 1948, there are two articles in particular on which it concentrates. The first of these is Article 2, which states: "everyone has the right to life, liberty, and security of person."

In 1950, in Britain, a man named Timothy Evans was found guilty of the murder of his daughter. Sixteen years later, the main witness at that trial, John Christie, was found to have committed a series of murders himself. His testimony against Evans no longer stood up in a court of law.

24

The frightened face of Timothy Evans, accused in 1950 of the murder of his daughter. Sixteen years later, Evans was cleared of the crime because of unreliable evidence. It was too late: he had been hanged for the murder. Amnesty International opposes the death penalty in all cases. Although 40% of death sentences have been commuted in recent years, execution is legal in more than one hundred countries.

Evans was granted a pardon. But it was too late: his punishment in 1950 was to hang.

What good did it do, discovering this man was innocent? What good is a posthumous pardon? And Timothy Evans is not the only one. In this century, in the United States alone, no less than twenty-three people have been put to death and then later found to be innocent.

There are times when Amnesty International is faced with a very difficult decision. It has to decide whether or not to take on cases of people who themselves may have abused human rights.

But in one situation, Amnesty feels that there is no difficult decision: the death penalty. There is no going back, no rectifying mistakes, once someone has been condemned to die. Amnesty opposes this punishment – whether it is by shooting, electrocution, lethal injection, hanging, stoning or decapitation – in every case. No matter what the person has done, the death penalty denies a person their basic right to life. To Amnesty, taking away a person's life, whether as crime or punishment, is wrong.

25

February 23, 1985: the public execution of ten convicted armed robbers in Nigeria. Being shot while tied to a barrel is just one of the ways the death penalty is carried out. Amnesty opposes all methods of execution. The bodies are roughly taken down in front of the thousands of people who have come to watch.

Don't leave me

"When I leave, my client begs me not to go. As the guards take him back to his cell, he often starts to cry." These words were spoken in 1989 by a death row lawyer in Alabama, USA, Bryan Stevenson. His client was fifteen years old.

In the USA you are not allowed to vote or to buy alcohol until you are eighteen; but you can be sentenced to death. Between 1985 and 1991, four people between the ages of twelve and seventeen were sentenced to death in America. By July 1991, there were thirty-one people under the age of eighteen on death row in twelve American states. Amnesty International states that the death penalty must be abolished no matter who is being sentenced or what their crime is. And it believes that sending children to their death is the greatest horror of all.

26

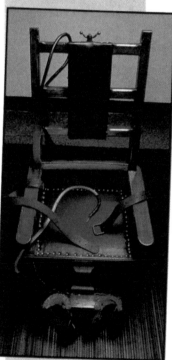

Below: Various forms of execution are in use in different countries. Pictured here is the electric chair, in use in the United States. The victim is strapped into the chair and a lethal current of electricity is passed through their body by means of electrodes.

Just let me live

Dalton Prejean was seventeen in 1978. In May of that year he was convicted of murdering a white policeman. Prejean was black, but the prosecutor excluded all black people from serving on the jury. The judge also moved the trial to a white area of Louisiana. The lawyer defending Prejean had never before handled a case for which the punishment would be the death sentence. Also, he was appointed by the court and not by the accused. It was Prejean's right to appoint his own lawyer to defend him, but he was too poor to do so. He might have got a fairer trial if he had. As it was, he was convicted by an all-white jury, with only an inexperienced lawyer on his side: the sentence was death.

There were plenty of other details to do with Prejean that should have been taken into account

27

Amnesty International

at his trial and were not. To start with, his lawyer never mentioned to the court that Prejean had been abused and neglected as a child; or that he had a history of mental illness and had been diagnosed as a schizophrenic. When he was only fourteen, he had been convicted of another murder and at that point, doctors had recommended that he be admitted to hospital for "a long stay". They had discovered some damage in his brain that caused him to lose control of his actions when he was under stress. This evidence never emerged at the trial. Doctors saw Prejean's need for help, but the court never heard about it.

We all make mistakes

The saddest thing of all is that the one fact that could not be hidden, his youth, was not used in his defence. No one said to the judge: "But he was only seventeen! He was still a child in the eyes of the law. Won't you give him the rest of his life to change?" The boy didn't ask for anything more. "I don't ask to get out of prison," he said. "I just ask to live with my mistake.... We all make mistakes in life." Amnesty felt that the jury who sentenced him answered one mistake with another. Even when Prejean appealed against his sentence, and the facts of his illness were made known, the state governor ordered his execution. After twelve years on death row, Dalton Prejean died in the electric chair on May 18, 1990.

Who can decide?

It is too late to decide that Timothy Evans was innocent, or that Dalton Prejean really should have had medical help instead of the electric chair. In the same year as Evans was hanged, a Japanese man named Sakae Menda was also sentenced to death for murder. In 1983, he was declared innocent and set free. He was lucky – or was he? For thirty-three years he had lived on death row, in the shadow of death. Sentenced prisoners wait on death row for their sentences to be carried out.

"The gallows is not only a machine of death but a symbol. It is the symbol of terror, cruelty and irreverence for life; the common denominator of primitive savagery, medieval fanaticism and modern totalitarianism."

Arthur Koestler,
Hungarian-born author.

28

Twenty-nine-year-old Dalton Prejean went to the electric chair in May 1990 for a crime he committed when he was seventeen. He first suffered the ordeal of twelve years on death row. In July 1991, there were thirty-one juvenile offenders on death row in the United States who were between fifteen and seventeen at the time of their crime. Amnesty campaigns particularly vigorously to abolish the death penalty for people under eighteen. In 1989, thirty-six countries abolished the death penalty. The year before, 2,229 people were executed in thirty-four countries.

Imagine what it must be like to live in the knowledge that at any moment, those footsteps outside your cell could be the guard coming to tell you that your time to die has come.

Amnesty believes the death penalty is wrong. Who can decide that another person should die? Amnesty's answer is: no one. And yet the death penalty is still legal in over one hundred countries including South Africa, Turkey and the countries that formerly made up the Soviet Union. Studies have shown that abolition of the death penalty does not lead to an increase in the rate of capital crime. Perhaps the most chilling criticism of this punishment are the words Amnesty published of executioner Albert Pierrepoint, "All the men and women I have faced at that final moment convince me that in what I have done I have not prevented a single murder."

One organization, even one as powerful as Amnesty, can hardly hope to combat such a widespread abuse of human rights, but Amnesty finds the answer in the individual. Amnesty is made up of individuals, each on their own as powerless as the prisoners they campaign for. Behind each campaign is one face and one story. The members of Amnesty pool their strength, and that is how Amnesty's battles are won.

29

Organizations that help the world: Amnesty International

by Marsha Bronson

Many organisations rely on voluntary public support. They therefore need to persuade people to see their point of view in order to gain public sympathy and backing. Amnesty International is a voluntary organisation working for human rights.

Read, Think and Write

1. Which Article of the United Nations' declaration does Amnesty believe supports their opposition to the death penalty?

2. How does the case of Timothy Evans back up Amnesty's argument against the death penalty? How do the photograph and the first sentence of the caption support this argument?

3. What examples does the writer give to support Amnesty's belief that sending children to their death is the greatest horror of all?

4. What is the difficult decision Amnesty is sometimes faced with and how does the case of Dalton Prejean link with this concern?

5. What arguments are put forward to support the idea that Prejean did not have a fair trial?

6. Why is Sakae Menda's luck questioned?

7. Who is Albert Pierrepoint? How is his quote a good conclusion to the argument against the death penalty?

8. How many countries still have a death penalty?

9. What other statistics does the text display to support the argument against the death penalty?

10. How does the layout of the extract help support Amnesty's point of view?

11. Are you persuaded by Amnesty's arguments against the death penalty? Write down your opinion of the arguments put forward in the extract.

Read and Analyse

1. Write a conversation between two people with opposing points of view. It could involve someone disagreeing with an Amnesty supporter's view of the death penalty, or you could choose your own subject to construct an argument around. Remember to use all the written conventions of speech.

Hint

Punctuation can be used to show someone's feelings – e.g. exclamation marks can indicate outrage.

2. Find and write a synonym and an antonym for each of the following words:
   (a) abolish
   (b) liberty
   (c) appeal
   (d) abuse
   (e) penalty
   (f) condemn

3. Write six sentences. In each sentence, use two words with opposite meanings.

> **Example**
> The <u>life</u> story of the famous actor was published after his <u>death</u>.

Read, Discuss and Act

1. In a small group make a list of as many other voluntary organisations as you can think of. Discuss whether you agree with their causes. How do their advertisements or literature try to persuade people to support them? Do the organisations fall into certain categories, such as overseas aid or animal welfare? Are there some that do not fit into particular categories?

2. Voluntary organisations often have 'flag days' to collect money. With a partner, role-play a short scene between a supporter collecting money and a passer-by in the street. Use the idea to develop different characters depending on the cause.

> **Example**
> An elderly person meets an old friend collecting for Help the Aged and this prompts a conversation about the good old days!

Pandora's box

Has TV lived up to people's expectations – whether good, bad or bo

Fifty-one years ago, the *Daily Mirror* warned its readers: "If you let a television set through your front door, life can never be the same again." How right it was. Now, thinking about the social impact of TV, it's easy to picture a *Royle Family* nation. But the true picture is far more complex. The medium has both influenced and reflected modern life – a situation that's unlikely to change in the digital, multi-channel, multiplatform future.

The BBC began the world's first regular high-definition television (HDTV) service from Alexandra Palace on 2 November 1936. Its first director-general, John (later Lord) Reith, generally acknowledged as the father of British public service broadcasting, instructed programme makers to "Educate, Inform, Entertain." At this time very few people owned or even had access to a television, but the medium was constantly being discussed in the press.

Live coverage of the Coronation of Queen Elizabeth II on 2 June 1953 – one of the earliest of many TV 'moments' that everyone just had to see – was a massive spur to receiver sales. In 1955

commercial television began in the UK, proving hugely popular despite being derided by Winston Churchill as "the tuppenny ha'penny Punch and Judy Show".

Mid to late 20th-century history became a series of crystallised TV images: the assassination and funeral of JFK (1963), the Moon landing (1969), Vietnam as the first 'TV war' (1964-73) and the fall of the Berlin Wall (1989).

Marshall McLuhan, the 'father of media studies', suggested that TV affects those who watch it and those who come in direct contact with it: "Jack Ruby shot Lee Oswald while tightly surrounded by guards who were paralysed by television cameras," he said. And his theory conveys the power of the medium as a whole.

Antisocial? Not b****y likely!

Well into the 1950s, some believed that TV would be like cinema, viewed on large screens in special theatres. By 1993, a report identified watching TV among the most popular home-based leisure pursuits of the previous 15 years, on a par with being with friends.

Other studies have highlighted the changing dynamic of families as each member vies for control of the remote. Mrs Whitehouse established the Viewers' and Listeners' Association in 1965 to protest against sex, violence and Alf Garnett; but, although links between TV and real-life antisocial conduct have long been sought, research has been inconclusive or contradictory.

TV's potential to turn us all into square-eyed couch potatoes has also caused concern. American sociologist Urie Bronfenbrenner

3 June 19
Mrs Mary
Whitehou
gives Tory
James Da
a bundle
366,355
signature
petitionin
"that the
be asked
to... prod
programm
which bui
character
instead o
destroyin

stated that TV prevents behaviour by glueing attention to the screen. In 1973, pop culture historian Asa Berger compared US television with drugs, saying people become hooked and sit there waiting for "something beautiful to happen".

However, TV has achieved some of the aims envisaged by Lord Reith. *Cathy Come Home* (1966) alerted people to the problem of homelessness; Gene Roddenberry always wove a moral into *Star Trek*; and modern British soap operas are often used to raise issues, frequently with a helpline number given out at the end of the episode.

Yet is TV the antisocial force that early critics feared? TS Eliot called it "A form of entertainment, which permits millions of people to listen to the same joke at the same time and yet remain lonesome." This neatly identifies TV as an isolating experience.

Anti-TV group White Dot, in the book *Get A Life*, calls television an anti-social, addictive drug and says that giving it up doubles people's free time. There's particular concern for children. A report

by the Independent Televis Commission says that homes children have an average of 2.6 sets and more than a third h one in the bedroom. The sur shows that 50 per cent of child watch TV before going to sch and 75 per cent switch on as s as they get home, and read only an average 15 minutes a

Is TV to blame? In her es *Television in the Home and Fa* (included in *Television – An I national History*), Susan Br notes that the family has chan for a number of reasons, not because of TV. Briggs furt points out that in 1960, pionee researcher Joseph Klapper refu to recognise a dichotomy betw the habits of "television famil and "non-television families".

So-called 'date TV', when vi ers make sure they're at home a certain programme, has alw given people a shared experie to discuss the next day, at worl in the playground. During 1950s and '60s respectively, *Quatermass* serials and the se *The Fugitive* cleared the stre

Beeb one

The mast and transmitting aerials at Alexandra Palace, London, in 1936, when the BBC began the world's first regular TV service

The television timeline: 1911-2001

1911 - the first electronic television principle is presented by AA Campbell-Swinton

1925 - John Logie Baird produces the first moving television pictures by using the Nipkow disc

1929 - the world's first regular TV

service is established by the Baird Television Company and the British Broadcasting Corporation

1936 - BBC starts the world's first HDTV service

1939-46 - BBC suspends broadcasts for duration of WWII

1953 - regular colour TV servi begin in the US

1955 - Independent commerc TV goes on air in the UK

1962 - TV signals are transmi over the Atlantic via Telstar

1967 - BBC2 goes colour

1973 - Teletext services begin

1980 - NHK demonstrates a

Telly it like it is... have we all become goggle-eyed couch potatoes like *The Royle Family* (above)? Did *Terror Of The Autons* (left) give you nightmares? Er, dunno – what's on tonight?

BBC PICTURE ARCHIVES ('92)

John Logie Baird is the most famous name in the history of TV technology, as he demonstrated both the first working system and, in 1928, colour TV pictures. Yet he is just a small part of the story.

Baird used a mechanical approach, a rotating disc invented in 1884 by Paul Nipkow, who developed the principles of television scanning But others favoured electronic approaches. In 1897 Karl Ferdinand Braun succeeded in producing narrow electron streams from cathode-ray tubes (CRT) that could trace patterns on fluorescent screens. Ten years later, Russian scientist Boris Rosing suggested the CRT as a TV receiver and produced crude geometrical patterns on a fluorescent screen.

Lines and pictures. Backed by RCA, V.K. Zworykin pursued an electronic solution. There was an initial collaboration with EMI's Research Laboratories but the head of EMI's research group, Isaac Shoenburg, was not convinced by the RCA system, which used 120 lines. Shoenburg proposed 405 lines at 50 frames per second, with interlaced scanning to give 25 pictures per second without flicker. The EMI team included the now-rediscovered genius Alan Dower Blumlein, also noted for his work on stereo and radar. The UK government gave the BBC permission to use both these standards and the overall EMI system, which formed the basis of the world's first regular HDTV service, started by the BBC in 1936.

Baird demonstrated colour TV pictures in 1928, but it wasn't until 1950 that the National Television System Committee (NTSC) ratified the 525 horizontal line/60 pictures per second standard, which is used throughout North America, Japan and parts of South America. Most of Europe adopted the 625/50 PAL (phase alternate line) system, and BBC2 began full colour services in 1967, followed by BBC1 two years later. France, eastern Europe and some African states use yet another system, known as SECAM (sequential colour and memory).

In 1973, Japanese state broadcaster NHK began work with manufacturers on higher definition TV. Japan developed the first prototype but lost out by sticking to analogue technology. Europe flirted with multiplex analogue components (MAC), but in 1993 recognised that the future was digital by establishing the Digital Video Broadcasting (DVB) project. As corny as the advertising tag-line was, in 1998 the future of television had indeed arrived.

August 1926: John Logie Baird with his first TV apparatus (imagine that in the corner of your living room!), which he presented to the Science Museum

PA NEWS

inspired endless conversa-s and dissections. In the early 0s, the *Dr Who* story *Terror Of Autons* was deemed so scary as discussed in Parliament.

tercooler discussions
has continued to the present who shot JR? (*Dallas*, 1980s), murdered Laura Palmer? *in Peaks*, 1990s) and the 'sum-of *Big Brother*' (2000) were watercooler TV', discussed at k and in the pub. This is despite e choice from multiple chan- and video (although Warner ne Video research shows that ten per cent of VCR owners their machines to record). he availability of so many nels could mean that people

aren't watching the same thing at the same time as often as they used to, but real 'event TV' still unites viewers around the water-cooler the following day.

"New technology won't strongly affect the notion of TV as a social technology," says Dr Annette Hill, reader in communications at the Centre for Communication and Information Studies. "People swap tapes, and having WAP or TV sets in bedrooms doesn't change the social aspect because people still discuss programmes at school or work. *Big Brother* caused a conver-gence of media, with newspapers picking up the story and people calling or texting each other to keep up with what was happening. Everything about it was social."

For further information
TV Living *by David Gauntlett and Annette Hill* (Routledge, £15.99)
Television – An International History, *edited by Anthony Smith (Oxford University Press, £16.99)*
Inventor of Stereo – Alan Dower Blumlein *by Robert Charles Alexander (Focal Press, £14.99)*
Get A Life! *by David Burke and Jean Lotus* (Bloomsbury, £12.99)

g prototype of the HiVision system
Channel 4 goes on air
satellite TV is introduced e UK
European Digital Video asting project initiated
175 channels go on air in with the start of digital

satellite; the first pay-per-view cable services start in the UK
1995 - Channel 5 goes on air in parts of the UK
1998 - digital TV begins in the UK
1999 - NTL launches TV-based interactive services on digital cable and digital terrestrial; Microsoft's WebTV is trialed in

London and Liverpool
2000 - interactivity becomes a reality, with Open on BSkyB; Kingston TLI begins tests of TV over ADSL
2001 - interactivity comes to digital terrestrial; broadcasters begin to investigate other forms of reception.

'Pandora's Box'

Focus magazine

An article in a magazine may include several different types of material. The extract on the previous pages is a special report on the effects of television on our lives. It gives some chronological facts about the development of television as well as some technical information and photographs to illustrate some of the points in the text. The writer also brings in some contrasting points of view about the effects television has on social behaviour.

1. What is the main point of the opening paragraph?

2. When did the BBC begin its television broadcasting service and what was the first instruction given to programme makers by John Reith?

3. When did commercial television begin and what was Winston Churchill's response?

4. What aims envisaged by Lord Reith has television achieved?

5. In what way did T. S. Eliot think that television was an antisocial force?

6. What is 'date TV' and what are its effects?

7. What is the chief point of the final paragraph in the main text? How does this link with the opening paragraph?

8. In what way is the programme 'The Royle Family' critical of TV?

9. What effect might the availability of an increasing number of channels have?

10. In two paragraphs write down your opinion of the views expressed in the article.

11. If you were researching the history of television, where might you find further information?

12. Write a factual account of the development of television in Britain.

Hint
Use the 'Television timeline' and 'Television technology' sections but remember you are writing about UK developments.

1. The writer uses a variety of sources to justify statements about the effects of television.

   (a) How many quotes does the writer use?

   (b) How many TV programmes are named?

(c) How many times are books or newspapers referred to?

(d) How many dates are given?

Write down an example of a quote, a TV programme, and a book or newspaper. After each one say what statement it refers to or supports.

2. Write a review of a television programme you have seen recently. You should give your opinion of its good and bad points.

Hint
Justify your opinion with references to features of the programme.

1. In a small group, discuss what TV programmes you enjoy. Do you make choices about what you view? Are there some programmes you have to switch off or do you just watch anything that is on? How much time do you spend watching television?

   Now discuss what you think the future of television will be. What sort of programmes do you think will remain popular?

2. In groups of two or three, role-play two or three different characters sitting on a sofa watching TV. Choose a programme you know and invent some characters to role-play. As you pretend to watch the programme comment on it in character so that different points of view are voiced.

   Example
   The scene could involve granddad, deaf Uncle Bob and a university student home on holiday, watching and commenting on a quiz show.

The indoor

Cats are adaptable but is it fair to deprive them of the great outdoors? In part one of our new series SARAH MORRIS looks at the arguments and finds there are both practical and emotive issues.

lif

There has been a gradual revolution in the way we keep our cats. From the free spirits they used to be, hanging around at all hours in streets, alleyways and gardens, many of them are now house-dwelling pets, born and bred.

It's a trend that's come from the United States and city-dwelling families, only to be adopted by UK owners, wherever their home might be.

The reasons are manifold, but decisions are made on a personal basis, often based on a painful experience of losing a cat on the road. Owners feel the need to protect and to hold on to the animal they invest so much love in for as long as they can.

In an ideal world there would be less traffic and drivers would be slower and more considerate. Each cat would have his own safe garden and neighbours would respect his right to roam.

But it is far from an ideal world, and just as owners use numerous arguments for keeping cats indoors, there are many ways in which a thoughtful person can ensure their cats lead an enjoyable and perfectly fulfilling life.

Human lifestyles and attitudes have changed. We are now more likely to live in towns and cities. Tolerance among humans living on top of one another is diminishing and we have become fearful in our own neighbourhoods.

Cats, typically viewed in a love 'em or hate 'em manner, are eliciting more extreme reactions among the 'don't likes' who wish to assert their rights.

Adapt-a-cat

One of the best things about cats as pets is that they are adaptable. They will happily live in small spaces and sometimes unlikely habitats, including trendy London lofts, and we can take advantage of that — to an extent. And, after all, there are several degrees of indoorness! Your cat could have access to a fenced-in back garden when you're outside in fine weather, have a fully enclosed garden, or purpose-built run attached to the house.

I would estimate that among those reading this article, up to half of you currently keep an indoor cat while a number are considering this way of life for your next cat. But it's not simply a case of keeping the back door shut — having an indoor cat is a big responsibility and with it come demands on your time, money and powers of creative thought.

6

More and more cats live purely indoors. Quality of life is all important for these pets.

Cat rights

In order to provide the best possible life for your indoor cats you will need to ensure you satisfy a number of basic requirements, as listed here.

* Good food, fresh water, places to sleep and a clean litter tray are needed, just as you would expect to provide any cat. For the indoor cat, the following are extra important:

* Company — if not human then of the feline or canine kind

* Space to run and play — with choices of sleeping places and areas to escape from other cats in the family

* Sun and air — all cats like to sunbathe, so warm sun streaming through a window will be much appreciated. Safe windows should allow him to breathe fresh air.

* Entertainment — a variety of toys to play with, alone and with you

* Scratching area — a place they can tear into as much as they like.

* Commitment — be aware you need to continually enrich their lives, providing them with new things to entertain (even if it is a large paper bag or box to play in).

You have to remember that your home is your cats' entire world. You will have to start thinking laterally and create new spaces for them. And you may have to forgo ideas of having a 'perfect home' because the top of your wardrobe may well be fitted out with a fleecy bed to become a high-up perch (a tree/shed roof substitute) and you'll need a scratch post or two (tree/fence substitute).

It's debatable whether you might want to continue the idea of entertainment to the extent of putting up a bird table or nesting boxes so puss has something to watch. Fish tanks on metal stands are asking for trouble!

Before you make the decision

There are pros and cons of keeping an indoor cat. Decide how these work for you and your own lifestyle — and your new cat. Is your home really the right environment for a cat? Perhaps you are creating more problems for yourself because of your location, and potential problems might be solved by moving to a property which would allow your cat to enjoy the outdoors in safety.

It's also important to select the right kitten. Some breeds are more energetic and demanding than others, but do be aware that temperament can vary between individuals. Take advice from breeders who will know their cats' temperaments and, because they keep cats indoors, can offer you the benefit of their experience.

Claire Bessant, chief executive of the Feline Advisory Bureau, has put together a list of pros and cons in her article on indoor cats in the latest issue of the FAB Journal. She urges cat owners to weigh up the risks and benefits of the indoor life. (See panel over the page.) ➤

7

The indoor life

111

PRACTICAL

These are common reasons for keeping cats indoors — all of them expressed in our recent survey.

Pros

● Traffic — no worries about cats being killed, injured, or causing an accident
● Less risk of infection and disease
● Owners' situation — ie in a flat which does not have access to the garden
● Less risk of theft (particularly if pedigree)
● Cats safe from possible attack by hooligans and airgun shootings
● No chance of straying and getting lost
● Better reactions from neighbours
● Large cat population locally already
● Dislike of cats hunting
● Persian cats' coats more easily kept in good condition
● No using neighbours' gardens as a toilet.
● Having peace of mind

Cons

● It's basically an unnatural lifestyle with a lack of opportunity to express natural behaviour
● There is a higher risk of a cat developing behavioural problems
● Owner has to make a lot of effort to ensure the cats don't become bored
● It's difficult to introduce a new cat to the household
● A greater risk of obesity
● Cats may be at risk of becoming over-dependent
● Owner has to maintain a litter tray
● Possible damage to carpets, curtains and furniture
● Boredom and curiosity could get a cat into trouble
● Should the cat escape, he will have no way of coping with what he encounters

predator. If it was a vegetarian it woul[...] like a rabbit!"

The FAB stance is that each person [...] make the decision based on their partic[...] circumstances and the nature of their c[...] Whatever you do, be sure your decisio[...] an informed one and one which you a[...] comfortable with.

Is it really fair?

Owners worry that they are being crue[...] the cats become bored? Is it fair on the[...] These are tricky questions to answer. F[...] very basic view, if introduced to this lif[...] kittenhood, they won't miss what they'[...] never known. But even then, there are [...] who will tell you about young kittens [...] are desperate to get outside, even thou[...] have never experienced it. "Sometimes [...] obvious that a cat is suffering from bei[...] kept inside, so you have to make a dec[...] to allow his freedom," Claire points ou[...]

In order for the cats not to become [...] you will need to put a lot of thought, t[...] and effort into keeping them amused.

"Having an indo[...] cat is a big responsibility..[...]

To reiterate, it has got to be your decision, based on your own feelings and your young cat's reactions. Be honest with yourself and look to the future. For example, if you have children, or are planning to have, it may be difficult to keep outside doors shut all the time. You'll need to be completely dedicated to your cats' needs, and willing to do this throughout their lives, not just through kittenhood.

"Some people can't bear the risk of having their cat run over," says Claire."But

personally I like them to go out if at all possible."

From time to time FAB receives calls from owners contemplating keeping an indoor cat. She warns them that owners will have to work hard at keeping their cats entertained and out of mischief.

Claire suggests owners remember the true nature of the cat. Whenever she takes calls from people who are distressed at their cats catching birds, she tells them: "Your cat looks and behaves like it does because it is a carnivore and 'top-of-the-chain'

An indoor cat should never be lonely. A well-matched pair of cats will be great company for one another.

Points to consider

on't try to convert a cat that has
iously had access to the outdoors. That
d be tantamount to cruelty.

umbers should be proportionate to the
of your house and the space you allow
n. Bear in mind cats are territorial
nals, so it's a good idea to start with the
ber you intend to keep and stick with
. It could be very difficult to introduce
cats to an established group. Be sure you
give each one the individual attention it
rves.

hink about your cats' natural needs and
ride facilities within the home which
fy them.

an your home before you get your new
n. Expect to buy (or make) scratch posts
climbing trees, and have lots of different
oys.

An owner's view

Paula Roberts decided that her next cats
would be indoor pets after tragically
losing two cats in one year. "I was
absolutely heartbroken that summer. Tim-
Tom, who was an outdoorsy, streetwise cat,
disappeared and was later found dead,
presumed poisoned, in a neighbour's
garden. We moved to another village and a
couple of months later my beloved
Abyssinian, Merlin, disappeared. He was a
very distinctive cat as he had a broken hip
and walked very awkwardly. And yet we
had no sightings, and to this day it breaks
my heart to think about losing him.

"I just couldn't go through all that again.
Merlin's hip had been broken when he was
knocked down by a car. And I'd had a
female Aby prior to him who was run over
and killed just outside our house.

"So, once we'd found a nice ground floor
flat, I bought two kittens and started again,
determined to keep them safe and sound
— for the whole of their natural lives.

"These two have made ideal indoor cats
and I've never had any problems with them.
They have a scratchpost/climbing frame
with a house to hide in. One of them,
Oliver, scratches at the carpet, but apart
from that they're absolutely fine."

And finally... be prepared to encounter
criticism from others. Indeed, many of
those with outdoor cats who completed our
survey said they thought that it was cruel or
selfish to keep indoor cats.

And yet, many of those who do have
indoor cats would, in their heart of hearts,
love to see their cats playing outside —
provided that they could do so safely.

Tell us about your experiences of keeping
cats indoors. How do you keep your cats

Owners are responsible for keeping their
indoor cats entertained. Left, a scratch post
and selection of toys are essential to prevent
boredom.

entertained? Do you have a cat room or
outdoor enclosure, or perhaps you have
custom-built an entertainment centre. This
article is part of a series and in the final part
we'd like to feature more 'real-life' indoor
cats and your stories. ■

he behaviourist's view

Cat pet
aviourist, Sarah
th says: "In an ideal
d, I would like all
to have access to
outside. But there
some very good
ons for keeping cats
ors, including busy roads,
ly populated urban areas,
so on. Some people seriously
ve that their cat would be at
outside.
There are lots of reasons why
le want to keep cats indoors
they can have a very high
ity of life.
But to express the full range
eir natural habits, cats should,
perfect world, be able to go
ide."

With regard to
breeds, the bottom line
is that it has been
proved possible to keep
all pedigree cats indoors.
But it's up to you, the
owner, to research the
temperament and needs
of the cat and provide a suitable
environment. Some breeds are
more demanding than others and
will become bored more quickly.
If you find out all you can from
breeders and invest some time
(and money) in creating a cat-
orientated home before your
kitten joins you, he will have lots
to keep him busy and you should
be able to avoid any problems.
Sarah says: "Breeds such as the
Abyssinian, Burmese and Siamese

can be kept indoors but you really
do have to work at it, while quieter
breeds such as the Persian are
usually quite happy to be inside."
She stresses that it is difficult
to generalise about pedigrees. "It's
a lot more to do with the way
they are socialised and housed
than their breed," Sarah explains.
"Moggies can be closer to their
wild natures, and sometimes
more 'streetwise'.
"If you want an indoor cat, get
a kitten so it can grow up
knowing nothing else. If you take
a cat from a rescue centre, even
though it is kept inside there, you
don't know if that cat has had
free access to the outdoors before."
Cats need places to hide, to
climb and toys that will help
them to exercise their natural
hunting instincts.

Though Sarah, like other
animal behaviourists, sees indoor
cats who display self-mutilation,
pica, and aggressive-type
behaviours, she says that there is
no scientific link between these
behaviours and an indoor life.
Instead, she says, it could point to
the fact that by definition, those
who have indoor cats are closer
to their animals and aware of
changes in behaviour and are also
more prepared to investigate
problems and find solutions.
"People who keep cats indoors
usually have very valid reasons
for doing so, and as long as some
of the reasons are for the welfare
of the cat, that's fine."

NEXT MONTH: We look at
the practical aspects of keeping
your indoor cat happy.

'The Indoor Life'

Your Cat magazine

Cats are such popular animals that many people not only enjoy keeping them as pets but like to read about them as well. The article you have just read is taken from a magazine which produces information especially for cat owners. Is it fair to keep a cat indoors? The article discusses this question and puts forward different points of view .

1. Where has the 'trend' for keeping indoor cats come from and what are the main reasons for this type of lifestyle for a cat?

2. What are the basic requirements of an indoor cat?

3. What does FAB stand for? Use quotes from the text to show what the chief executive of this organization feels about indoor cats.

4. Why has cat owner Paula Roberts decided to keep her cats indoors?

5. What is the behaviourist's view of pedigree cats as indoor cats?

6. How might 'moggies' be different from pedigree cats in their responses to an indoor lifestyle?

7. How do the pictures show aspects of the argument for keeping indoor cats?

8. Which of the points in the 'Pros' section of the survey do you think are the most important in an argument for cats to be kept indoors?

9. Which of the points in the 'Cons' section of the survey do you think are the most important in an argument against keeping cats indoors?

10. Write a speech you might make to support the view that cats should be kept indoors, or one against the idea.

11. Write about being kept indoors from the point of view of the cat.

Hint
Think about the character of the cat you are pretending to be. Are you a 'moggie' or a pedigree?

114

Read and Analyse

1. Write the root word and suffix of the following words. Write the meaning of the root word and then write another word which has the same suffix as each word in the list.
   - (a) adaptable
   - (b) distinctive
   - (c) commitment
   - (d) laterally
   - (e) potential
   - (f) personal
   - (g) proportionate
   - (h) behaviourist

2. Write ten questions to be used in a survey to gain an idea of readers' responses to the debate in the article.

Read, Discuss and Act

1. Many different wild animals are now kept as domestic pets. Do you think this is against the rights of these animals? Do you think animals should have rights? Do we need zoos and wildlife parks?

2. In small groups, plan and present a quiz show entitled 'Animal World'. Prepare some questions and answers. Role-play the contestants and the questioner. Try not to have too many weak links!

Superhumans

Like it or not, in a few short years we'll have the po

Illustrations: Chris Draper

IF YOU put your ear to the tracks, you can hear the train coming.

In conference halls around the world, geneticists and developmental biologists have been gathering to discuss what once was unthinkable—genetically engineering human embryos so that they, and their children, and their children's children, are irrevocably changed. These experts are talking with remarkable candour about using germ-line engineering to cure fatal diseases or even to create designer babies that will be stronger, smarter, or more resistant to infections.

Doctors are already experimenting with gene therapy, in which a relatively small number of cells—in the lungs, say—are altered to correct a disease. Germ-line engineering, however, would change every cell in the body. People would no longer have to make do with haphazard combinations of their parent's genes. Instead, genetic engineers could eliminate defective genes, change existing ones or even add a few extra. Humanity would, in effect, take control of its own evolution.

So awesome is this idea, that until a year or so ago, the taboo on human germ-line engineering was absolute. But opinions have started to shift. Once barely considered a topic for polite conversation among even the most gung-ho of geneticists, germ-line engineering of humans is becoming so much grist to the mill of scientists gossiping around the coffee pot.

Not that the pillars of the scientific establishment agree on this emerging technology, not by a long way. In a straw poll, researchers variously described the idea of human germ-line engineering as "irresistible", "morally questionable" or just plain "dangerous". What they did agree on is that germ-line engineered humans are likely to become a reality. Tampering with a human embryo to create changes that can be passed from one generation to the next is still more or less *verboten*—23 countries have signed a Council of Europe convention that bans it, and officials at the US Food and Drug Administration promise not to give the go-ahead without much public deliberation. Despite this, however, most experts say they'd be surprised if designer babies are not toddling around within the next 20 years or so.

Gregory Stock, a biophysicist-turned-expert on technology and society at the University of California, Los Angeles, helped to organise a symposium in March called "Engineering the Human Germline". The task? Not to look way into the future, but at what we'll be faced with in the next decade or two. "There is no way to avoid this technology," explains Stock, who thinks that calling the evolutionary shots will create a happier, healthier society. "The knowledge is coming too fast, and the possibilities are too exciting."

Public enthusiasm could soon match Stock's: poll after poll shows that a sizeable minority of parents—sometimes as many as 20 per cent—say that they see nothing wrong with genetically altering their children for health reasons, to give them an edge over the child at the next desk—or even to stop them being homosexual.

So what is shifting the mind-set about human germ-line engineering from "never" to "well, maybe"? The main driving force, most experts agree, is the new technologies rolling inexorably along the tracks. We are discovering not only what our genes do, but how to make precise changes in them. And although the human genome isn't yet completely sequenced, already the databases contain

3 October 1998

25

details of thousands of genes, and of thousands of variations within them, along with information about how these variations affect physical and emotional traits. Added incentive comes, paradoxically, from frustrations with gene therapy.

Gene therapy promised to cure genetic disorders such as cystic fibrosis and sickle-cell anaemia, and even common illnesses such as cancer. But although the glitches are slowly being fixed, few people have so far benefited from the procedure. The problem is getting new genes into enough cells, and keeping them there for long enough to do any good.

With germ-line engineering you have to tweak only one cell—a fertilised human egg—which is "infinitely easier", says Leroy Hood, a molecular biologist at the University of Washington in Seattle. "We have terrific ways to do that." Once a genetic engineer has changed the genome of an egg fertilised in a lab dish, the egg divides over and over again, forming all the tissues of the body. Every cell will have exactly the same genetic make-up as the altered egg.

Now and forever

Genetically engineered mice and farm animals have been around for years and are used for everything from basic research to attempts to create "humanised" animal organs for transplant. But what might be considered a bonus in agricultural biotechnology—the fact that any changes are present in the animal's sperm and eggs (the "germ cells") and so will be passed on to succeeding generations—is for many the most worrying thing about genetic engineering in humans. The critics point out that if medicine has played a bit part in our recent evolution—antibiotics, for example, allow people with less than robust immune systems to survive long enough to pass this trait into the next generation—genetic engineering has the potential to be a star performer.

One reason for cold feet is that large-scale genetic engineering could actually rob society of desirable traits. What if the "disease" genes in combination with other genes, or in people who are merely carriers, also help produce such intangibles as artistic creativity or a razor-sharp wit or the ability to wiggle ones ears? Wipe out the gene, and you risk losing those traits too. And while no one would wish manic depression on anyone, society might be the poorer without the inventiveness that many psychologists believe is part and parcel of the disorder. In his book *Remaking*

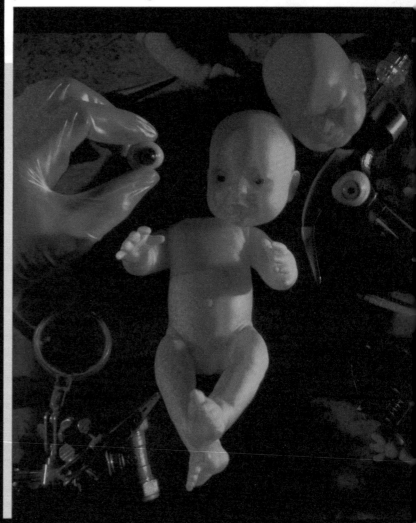

'What if the disease genes, with other gen[e] produce intangibles such as artistic creati[

Eden, Lee Silver, a biologist at Princeton University, goes as far as to suggest that a century or two of widespread engineering might even create a new species of human, no longer willing or able to mate with its "gene poor" relations ("Us and them", *New Scientist*, 9 May, p 36).

"The potential power of genetic engineering is far greater than that of splitting the atom, and it could be every bit as dangerous to society," says Liebe Cavalieri, a molecular biologist at the State University of New York in Purchase. Cavalieri, who has worked in the field for more than 30 years, thinks it unlikely that the ugly side of genetic engineering will stop development of the technology in its tracks. "It is

virtually inevitable it will get used and for the most banal reasons possible—to make some money, or to satisfy the virtuoso scientists who created the technology."

If esoteric worries about what may or may not happen in a genetically engineered society are unlikely to change people's views, safety issues could—at least until they are solved. "There is a real risk of unforeseen, unpredictable problems," says Nelson Wivel, deputy director of the Institute for Human Gene Therapy at the University of Pennsylvania, and former executive director of the National Institutes of Health Recombinant DNA Advisory Committee. In gene therapy, genes are ferried into cells by modified

118

**eople who are merely carriers, also help
arp wit or the ability to wiggle your ears?
e out the disease genes, and you risk
ng those traits as well'**

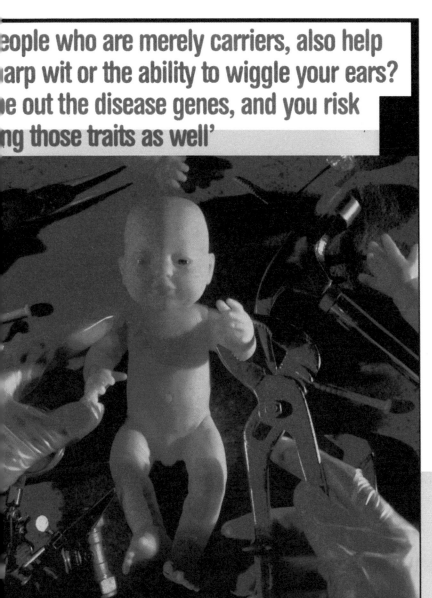

viruses or other means. It's a risky business, because genes can get inserted in the wrong spot in the genome, killing the cell outright or, far worse, triggering cancer. But at least with gene therapy there is natural damage control—few cells pick up the genes even when the procedure goes well, cancer only affects one individual, and, as the procedure has always been carried out long after birth, there's no chance of upsetting key developmental genes.

With germ-line engineering, on the other hand, there's more scope for unpredictable, even monstrous, alterations. Take the so-called "Beltsville pig". This pig, a thorn in the side of high-tech agriculturists and an icon for animal rights activists

everywhere, was engineered by scientists at the US Department of Agriculture to produce human growth hormone that would make it grow faster and leaner. The engineers added a genetic switch that should have turned on the growth hormone gene only when the pig ate food laced with zinc. But the switch failed. The extra growth hormone made the pig grow faster, but it also suffered severe bone and joint problems and was bug-eyed to boot. Of course, unlike human experiments, slaughtering "failures" is always an option for animal genetic engineers.

Before genetic engineering of humans can become a reality, each candidate gene and its switches would need to be

extensively studied in animals first, and any changes would have to be made with a surgical precision that reduced the chances of a "Beltsville human" to just about zero. As it happens, over the past few years, molecular geneticists have been busily developing the tools to do just this sort of "genetic surgery".

For years, genetic engineers have altered farm animals by injecting genes into fertilised eggs and then placing them in an animal's womb. But the technique is far too unreliable to use in humans. Out of every 10 000 eggs injected, roughly three make it to adulthood with the gene functioning as planned. What's more, it is possible only to add whole genes, not to fine-tune existing ones.

With mice, the process is more refined. Mice embryos contain embryonic stem (ES) cells that will grow and divide in a flask. That allows the engineers to make use of "homologous recombination", the process by which DNA strands bind to, and sometimes replace, DNA strands of similar sequence. With homologous recombination it is possible to make tiny, surgically precise changes within genes, with the technique depending in part on being able to sort through a large number of ES cells, only picking out the ones that have taken the genetic change in the correct place. Those cells are then added back to an embryo, where they can form any part of the animal. The result is a "chimera", an animal whose body contains both normal and altered cells. To create an animal with the altered gene in every cell, a chimera with the change in its eggs is bred with one that has the change in its sperm—one reason the technique can't be used in humans.

But the efficiency of gene surgery is improving so that fewer cells are needed to start with. That has made it possible for several labs to try gene surgery directly on fertilised mouse eggs, says Dieter Gruenert, a molecular geneticist at the University of California, San Francisco, who is developing just such a technique. The process is still in its infancy, but it could one day make it possible to genetically engineer human eggs, eliminating the need for crossbreeding.

A more immediate solution will probably come from an alternative way of generating lots of identical embryonic cells: the technology that produced Dolly & Co.

Cloning relies on a combination of two new techniques. First, grow cells taken from an adult or an embryo in a flask under conditions that encourage them to

'Superhumans'

***New Scientist* magazine**

For the past few years genetic engineering has been an issue that has caused considerable debate. Some of those issues are raised in the piece of writing you have just read, an extract from an article which appeared in the *New Scientist*.

Read, Think and Write

1. What does the writer's opening sentence mean in this context?

2. In what way might germ-line engineering be used, according to experts?

3. How would germ-line engineering be different from the gene therapy doctors are already experimenting with?

4. How does the writer show that the scientific establishment is not in agreement on the emerging technology?

5. What is stopping the possibility of designer babies toddling around at the moment?

6. What is Gregory Stock's opinion on the issue?

7. How does the writer use references to public opinion in the article?

8. What do the human genome databases contain?

9. What might the 'disease' genes in combination with other genes produce and how might this affect society?

10. The writer weaves the arguments for and against the development of genetic engineering into the article. Write examples from the text under the headings 'For' and 'Against'.

Hint
Use the quotes from various people.

Read and Analyse

1. Use a dictionary and the context of the article to write down the meaning of the following words and phrases:
   (a) remarkable candour
   (b) haphazard combinations
   (c) eliminate defective genes
   (d) added incentive
   (e) paradoxically
   (f) intangibles

Hint
Which person seems to have a more positive view of genetic engineering?

2. Use the conventions of script writing to write the script of a television interview with Gregory Stock and Nelson Wivel. Construct your questions and answers around their quotes and the information in the article to help you decide what they might be asked in the interview.

3. Do you think the images in the illustrations help the argument for genetic engineering? Write about the design and layout of the article. In your analysis, include comment on how they might influence opinions about genetic engineering.

Read, Discuss and Act

1. In a small group, discuss what you think the future outcome of genetic engineering might be. Do you feel positive about it or concerned? Will parents want designer babies? What might a designer baby be like? Who will decide what are good traits and bad traits?

2. In a small group, role-play a scene which will involve medical technology in some way. It could be a dentist dealing with a nervous patient or an emergency in the casualty department of a hospital.

Acknowledgements

The author and publishers would like to thank the following copyright holders for permission to reproduce the extracts used in this book:

Abigail's Party and *Arms and the Man* publicity leaflets are reproduced by permission of Method and Madness.

Article by Dennis Rice in the *Sunday Express* is reproduced by permission of Express Newspapers Ltd. Photographs © Barbados Beach Club and Connors Picture Agency.

Article by John Lichfield, Stephen Castle and Michael McCarthy and cartoon by Tim in the *Independent* are reproduced by permission of Independent Newspapers Ltd. Photograph © Reuters/Popperfoto.

Extracts from *The Crime and Mystery Book* by Ian Ousby, published by Thames and Hudson, are reproduced by permission of The Andrew Lownie Literary Agency on behalf of the estate of Ian Ousby. Illustration on p.112 © The Pulp Archive. Illustrations on pp.111 and 113 by David Johnson.

Extract from *War Boy* by Michael Foreman is reprinted by permission of Pavilion Books. Puffin Books edition published by Penguin Books.

Extract from *Cider with Rosie* by Laurie Lee, published by Hogarth Press, is used by permission of The Random House Group Limited.

Extract from *The Diary of Samuel Pepys*, edited by Robert Latham and William Matthews, is reproduced by permission of HarperCollins Publishers Ltd.

Extract from *Around the World in 80 Days* by Michael Palin is reproduced with the permission of BBC Worldwide Limited. Copyright © Michael Palin 1992.

Extract from *Roald Dahl* by Jeremy Treglown is reproduced by permission of Faber and Faber Ltd.

Extracts from *Manchester United Annual 2002* by Adam Bostock are reproduced by permission of Carlton Books Ltd and Manchester United Plc.

Extract from David Attenborough's *The Atlas of the Living World* by Dr Philip Whitfield, Dr Peter D. Moore and Professor Barry Cox is reproduced by permission of Marshall Editions Ltd. Illustrations by: pp.12–13 (*t* to *b*) Ed Stuart, Michael Woods, Ed Stuart; pp.16–17 Dave Ashby. Photograph on p.17 © Oxford Scientific Films/R. Villarosa.

Extract from *Horrible Science: Vicious Veg*, text © Nick Arnold 1998, first published by Scholastic Books Ltd, reproduced with permission.

Extract from the Toshiba Satellite Quickstart Manual is reproduced by permission of Toshiba Information Systems (UK) Ltd.

Extract from *Water Garden Design* by Yvonne Rees and Peter May is reproduced by permission of Quarto Publishing plc. Photographs © Dave Bevan (108TR, 109 CR), Garden Picture Library/Steven Wooster (108T, 110 TL), Harry Smith Collection (111 TR).

Extract from 'Fantastic effects in Photoshop' in *Computer Arts* magazine is reproduced by permission of Future Publishing. © *Computer Arts* 1999. (*Computer Arts* website: www.computerarts.co.uk)

Extract from *Food of the Sun* by Alistair Little and Richard Whittington (£9.99 Paperback) is reproduced by permission of Quadrille Publishing.

Extracts from *Delia Smith's Winter Collection* (copyright © Delia Smith 1995) and *Flavours of India* (copyright © Madhur Jaffrey 1995) are reproduced with the permission of BBC Worldwide Limited.

Extract from *The Return of the Naked Chef* (copyright © Jamie Oliver 2000), published by Michael Joseph, is reproduced by permission of The Penguin Group (UK).

Advertisement for Perrier is reproduced by permission of Perrier Vittel UK Ltd.

Adverisement for Chief Executive to Coventry City Council is reproduced by permission of PricewaterhouseCoopers.

WWF letter and questionnaire are reproduced by permission of WWF-UK.

Extract from *Organizations that help the world: Amnesty International* by Marsha Bronson is used by permission of Exley Publications Ltd. Photographs © Popperfoto, Camera Press, Frank Spooner Picture Agency and Associated Press.

Article entitled 'Pandora's Box' by Kevin Hilton is reproduced courtesy of *Focus* Magazine © National Magazine Company. Photographs © BBC Picture Archives and PA News.

Article entitled 'The indoor life' by Sarah Morris is reprinted by permission of *Your Cat* magazine.

Extract from article entitled 'Superhumans' by Robert Taylor is reproduced by permission of *New Scientist*. Illustrations © Chris Draper.

Every effort has been made to trace copyright holders and to obtain their permission for the use of copyright material. The author and publishers will gladly receive information enabling them to rectify any error or omission in subsequent editions.